Praise for *Gabriel*

No Christmas tree will ever look the same again after you have read Randall Bush's piece of Christmas magic. Among the branches of this familiar tree he creates a whole world of good, evil and salvation. Echoes of John Bunyan, C. S. Lewis and the Bible abound, as do humorous side-swipes at the absurdities of our present-day world, but it is the author's own vivid imagination that will keep the young reader turning the page. Randall Bush tells a good story, and I commend it as a way of sharing in the best story of love.

—PAUL S. FIDDES
D.Phil (Oxford), D.D. (Oxford)
Principal Emeritus
and Professional Research Fellow
Regent's Park College, Oxford

The family is delighted with [Gabriel's Magic Ornament]; I have re-read it; and a thirteen-year old church friend said that she could not put it down! A delightful fantasy tale, that carries the reader along within a world comparable with that of C. S. Lewis's Narnia books. It conveys an unobtrusive spiritual dimension, but will also en-trance most especially young readers of between eight and fourteen, and will also be enjoyed by readers of all ages. The book is an ideal gift for children, especially at the Christmas season.

—DR. ANTHONY C. THISELTON
Emeritus Professor of Christian Theology
University of Nottingham, England
Canon Theologian of Leicester Cathedral
and of Southwell Minster

Praise for *Gabriel's Magic Ornament*

A Christmas tale destined to become a classic! Oxford graduate Randall Bush continues in the tradition of Lewis Carroll, J. R. R. Tolkien, and C. S. Lewis in his ability to create a world of imagination.

—DR. HARRY L. POE
Former Program Director
C. S. Lewis Summer Institute, Oxford

GABRIEL'S MAGIC
ORNAMENT

GABRIEL'S MAGIC ORNAMENT

Randall Bush

D.Phil., University of Oxford

BORDERSTONE PRESS, LLC

2011

Second American Edition

Gabriel's Magic Ornament

Author: Randall Bush

Cover Art and Title Page: D. Ellen Kay

Published by BorderStone Press, LLC,
PO Box 1383, Mountain Home, AR 72654
Dallas, TX - Memphis, TN

www.borderstonepress.com

Copy editor: Rachel Mooney
Supervising editor: Brian Mooney

ISBN: 978-1-936670-23-9

Library of Congress Control Number: 2011942706

Interior is acid free and lignin free.
It meets all ANSI standards for archival quality paper.

For my wonderful wife, Cindy,

the mother of my children

CHAPTERS

—Chapter One—

ORNAMENT OF DREAMS, AND DREAMS OF ORNAMENTS

CHRIS WIPED THE FOG from the window and looked outside. Snow still blanketed the ground and ice-coated tree branches still clattered in the wind like skeletons. Nothing had changed since ten minutes earlier, and he had been back and forth to the window all morning.

He should have been glad that school was cancelled. He would have been overjoyed if he had succeeded in convincing his mother to let him go outside and play. Unfortunately, because she had said "no" at least three times, he was down in the mouth. And when he asked her if he could open just one Christmas present, since Christmas was still several weeks away, she would not agree to let him do that either. Just then, he caught sight of some neighbor children sliding down an icy hill on an old hubcap.

"Mom, look!" he said. "Lots of kids are out there playing. Why can't I? Please let me go outside! Please!"

"What did I already tell you?" she asked.

"I don't remember," he answered, hanging his head.

"Well I do, and I'm getting tired of having to repeat the word. But since you didn't seem to hear me the first three times, I am going say it again. 'No', 'no', 'no'! Now, if you don't understand the meaning of that word, maybe I'll have to help you learn it by sending you straight to your room for the rest of the day."

He hung his head and grumbled, "You never let me do anything."

"Chris, can't you see we're in the middle of an ice storm?" she asked. "I'm not going to let you go out there and catch your death of cold, or worse, let you break an arm or a leg and ruin your Christmas."

His mother left him to sulk as she went to the kitchen to finish making dinner. Meanwhile, his sister Laura walked into the room and saw him sitting there looking like he had lost his best friend.

"What's wrong with you?" she asked.

"Mom won't let me go outside and play."

"That's okay. You can stay inside and play house with me," she offered.

Chris shot an angry, disgusted look at her. "I can't think of anything more boring than playing house with a goofy girl."

Laura burst into tears and ran to tell her mother. In a moment Mom returned with Laura.

"Alright," she said. "Apologize to your sister this minute. She was only trying to cheer you up, and look how you've treated her."

"I'm sorry," Chris said halfheartedly. He stared out the window again and sighed, "When will Dad be home?"

"He'll be a bit late. He had to stop and get a new string of lights for the Christmas tree on his way from work. He's got to replace that burned-out one on the bottom branch." She looked at the Christmas tree and said, "Good grief! I hope your father doesn't buy any more ornaments for that tree. It's so overloaded now it's ready to topple over." Mother went to the kitchen and started bringing out plates and utensils to set the table for dinner. "Chris," she said, noticing that he had not moved from the window, "why don't you try reading until your father gets home? There is a book on that shelf about Christmas I know you haven't read."

Chris decided his mom might be right, so he went to the shelf and found a book entitled, *A Brief History of Christmas*. He was just getting interested in it when a car door slammed. "Dad's home!" he shouted, jumping up and tossing the book aside. As he darted to the door, Laura joined him. When they opened it, they saw Dad bundled in a heavy coat and overloaded with shopping bags. The children immediately latched on to his arms like spider monkeys, and Mom, pushing on the door, finally managed to shut out the howling, freezing wind. Dad let out a "brrr" and shivered as he set down the bags. The children wasted no time rummaging through them.

"That weather is just awful," he said, taking off his cap and shaking pellets of sleet out of it. "It looks like we're going to be iced in for a while. It's a good thing we bought groceries yesterday."

"Did you have any trouble on the roads?" Mom asked.

"No, but they're starting to get really treacherous," he replied. "I saw several cars skidding off."

"Well, I'm glad you made it home safely, dear. Were you able to stop at the store and get the lights?" she asked.

"Yes," Dad replied. "I hate that we're going to have to take all the ornaments off the tree just to replace that one burned-out string. That will be such a mess."

"Speaking of ornaments," said Mom. "You didn't..."

"Didn't what?"

"Buy any more?"

Dad blushed as Laura lifted the evidence from the bag. "Look, Mama! Isn't it pretty?"

"You really are something," Mom remarked. "When it comes to decorating for Christmas, you're worse than a child!"

"I couldn't very well pass it up." Dad's face glowed like an excited little boy. He took the beautiful but tarnished golden angel ornament from Laura's hand and held it up in the light. "This is a rare jewel if ever there was one. I found it in that old Christmas shop in town. You know the one I'm talking about—that shop in the square. I really tried hard to resist the urge to go in because I know what a sucker I am for unusual Christmas ornaments. Honest, I really did try to stop myself, but I just couldn't help it. Something kept calling me, 'Come in! Come in the shop!' I swear it was this ornament calling me. I think I must have been hypnotized."

Mom smiled. All she could say was, "Really?"

"Yes," Dad said. "Inside sat an old man who looked like he could have been Santa Claus's twin brother. Before I knew it, I was paying him for this magic ornament."

"Magic, indeed," Mother said. "We can hear all about it later. Dinner's already on the table, and we don't want our food to get cold."

"Mom's right," Dad said. "We'll eat first. Then I'll tell you kids all about the magic ornament when we're finished."

After dinner, Chris grabbed the ornament, jumped up from the table, and ran to the sofa.

"Let me hold it, too," Laura begged, following him.

"Okay," Dad said. "Don't fight over it, or I won't be able to tell you my story. First, let's help Mom clear the table."

Without a fuss, the children quickly jumped up and helped their mother and father clear off the dishes and clean the kitchen. But the moment they were finished, they anxiously grabbed Dad by his arms and pulled him over to the sofa.

"Okay, kids," he said. "Let's sit down, and I'll tell you my story about our new magical angel ornament."

"Is it really magical, Daddy?" Laura asked.

"I'm pretty sure it is," he said. "It's called Gabriel's Magic Ornament, and there's not another like it in the whole world."

"How do you know?" Laura asked.

"The shopkeeper who looked like Santa Claus's twin brother told me," said Dad. "He claimed that merchants from Israel sold it to him, and that they got it from an old, old, old church in the little town of Bethlehem."

Mom, who was finishing up in the kitchen, rolled her eyes. She figured her husband was coming up with yet another of his unbelievable stories.

"An old, old, old church, huh?" Chris commented. He had a skeptical look on his face.

"Yes," said Laura. "In the little town of Bethlehem!" She belted out "O Little Town of Bethlehem," trying to sound like an opera singer.

"Okay, if you're going to act silly," said Dad, "I just won't bother telling you the rest of the story."

"I'm sorry, Daddy," Laura piped. "Please tell it to us. We'll try to be good."

"Anyway, as I was saying," Dad continued, "this ornament is one of a kind. And it has hung on the Christmas trees of many very famous people."

"Like who?" asked Laura.

"Kings and emperors, of course."

"That's interesting?" Chris said, still looking skeptical. "So how did such a famous ornament wind up here?"

Laura could hardly contain a snicker.

"Don't be too hard on your father now, children," Mom said with a tone of sarcasm. "You know how sensitive he is about his stories."

"Thank you, Mother," Dad said, pretending to have his feelings hurt. "I'll say it again—famous people such as 'kings and emperors.'"

"Then that ornament must be pretty expensive," Chris guessed.

Mom turned her head toward Dad, who caught a glimpse of her face out of the corner of his eye.

"Well, I'd rather not talk about that." Dad had hoped the topic of how much the ornament cost would not come up, and he quickly changed the subject. "Anyway, as I was saying, the old shopkeeper claimed the ornament was made from gold brought by the Wise Man, Balthazar, to the Christ Child."

"I hope that ornament isn't made of real gold," Mom stated.

Dad ignored her.

"Did the Wise Man make it?" asked Laura.

"No. It was made by the Bishop of Myra."

"How much did that ornament cost?" Mom wanted to know.

"I got a good deal on it," said Dad. "Yes, Laura, the Bishop of Myra," he repeated.

"Who is that?" Laura asked.

"I don't know," he answered. "However, the shopkeeper said the ornament was magic because the Bishop of Myra made it."

"How good of a deal?" Mom pressed.

Dad kept ignoring her. "First, you have to hang it on the tree," he told the children. "Whoever hangs it will have an exciting Christmas dream! The strange thing is that the ornament disappears once the dream is over and then mysteriously appears in the old church in Bethlehem where it came from. The merchants who sold it to the shopkeeper claimed this has happened hundreds of times."

"I hope for your sake it doesn't disappear," Mom told Dad, "because if it cost as much as I suspect it did, you will have to take it back as soon as this ice storm is over."

"Oh, Mom!" the children cried. They begged her to let them hang it on the tree, just to see what would happen.

"Is it okay, Mother?" Dad asked.

She didn't answer but just walked back into the kitchen.

"Okay, children," said Dad. "You go ahead and hang the ornament. I'll bet it won't really disappear as the old shopkeeper claimed it would. Then we can take it back like Mama said, and everybody will be happy."

"Please, Daddy, can I hang it?" asked Laura.

"No, I want to do it!" shouted Chris.

"Don't argue, children. You can both hang it." Dad walked with the children over to the Christmas tree. "Laura, you hold on to one wing, and Chris, you hold on to the other. Hang the ornament on that bottom branch. If nothing happens, we'll know it's not really magic. Then I'll tell the shopkeeper that it didn't do what he said and demand a refund."

* * *

The moment the angel ornament touched the tree, everything went black. Then a brilliant light flashed, forcing their eyelids shut. When they managed with some difficulty to open them, they saw the ornament closing in on them. They tried to let go of it, but they could not. It held them firmly in its grasp. Suddenly, their arms started being sucked into it. Like a genie emerging from a lamp, it started changing into something huge and monstrous. Its face became enormous and frightening. The ornament was changing into a terrifying but beautiful angel. So tightly now did it hold them in its grip that they felt paralyzed. Next, the angel's body began to swirl like a whirlpool, rotating more and more swiftly until it sucked them under completely.

"Let me go!" shouted Laura. "Chris, I'm scared! Chris, where are you?"

"Over here!" he screamed, but the wind was howling so fiercely it drove their words back into their mouths. The angel grew more brilliant and its pull became so strong, they felt as if they were caught in the gravitational field of the sun. They struggled to break free but were helpless to escape its clutches.

"Mom! Dad! Help!" Laura shouted. She could barely hear Chris crying out for them, too, but as far as their parents were concerned the children's pleas went unheard and unanswered.

They were now so far down in the whirlpool of light that they could no longer see where they had come from or where they were going. They could only feel themselves accelerating. Eventually, Laura managed to reach out, find her brother's arm, and latch on to it. Once she got hold of him, she managed to wrap her arms around him and to hold on to him for dear life.

Suddenly they saw lightning flashing and heard thunder roaring. They were coming to the other end of the vortex. Beneath their feet, they could now see the branches of their Christmas tree turning into roads. Pine needles started piling up to form hills and valleys. Strings of lights were becoming bridges that crossed great gorges, connecting lower roads to higher ones.

"Chris! We're going to crash! We're going to die!" Laura screamed.

"Hang on, Laura!" he shouted. "Pray for a safe landing!"

The roads, hills, and valleys continued to expand until— plop—the children landed in their midst. The angel had vanished without warning and was now nowhere to be seen.

The children stood up, uninjured but very much shaken by their fall.

"How do you like that?" Chris remarked. "I guess that answers our question about the angel ornament being magical."

Low hills and valleys stretched before them. Above were lacy, greenish clouds with brown paths running through them, but the clouds did not drift the way clouds normally do.

"Where are we?" Laura asked.

"With that tornado we just went through?" said Chris. "My first guess would be that we're in the Land of Oz...or maybe the Twilight Zone. But seeing the tree branches and strings of lights makes me think that we're really inside our Christmas tree."

Just then they heard a terrible commotion. Loud snorting and vicious barking sounds whizzed past their ears like fast balls coming from just over one of the hills.

"That sounds scary," Laura said. "Maybe we'd better get away from here before whatever that is finds us."

"We can hide in those bushes and check it out from there," Chris said.

"But it sounds like some kind of a monster," Laura said. "What if it tries to eat us?"

"I promise I'll protect you," Chris reassured her.

They climbed almost to the top of the hill, and then crawled on their knees the rest of the way until they could see over the crest. They hid behind bushes so that whatever it was would not see them.

"Look," Chris said. "It's only a pig and a dog on the road. They're fighting over something, but what, I wonder?"

"Are those baskets they're carrying?" asked Laura.

"Look, the pig has an apple in his hand," Chris said. "So that's what they're fighting over—apples!"

Just then, the dog knocked the basket out of the pig's hand and apples tumbled everywhere. Frantically, the pig grabbed its basket and began shoveling the apples back into it. Meanwhile, the dog managed to steal one of the pig's spilt apples and stick it into his own basket. When the pig saw it, he let into the straggly mutt with fierce oinks and squeals.

"Good grief," Chris whispered. "Look at them go. I haven't seen a fight this good since Dad took me to the wrestling matches."

Just then, light flashed on the ground around them followed by a clap of thunder.

"Oh, no!" cried Laura. "The tornado is back!"

They covered their heads, but nothing happened. Then a deep fog formed slowly and quietly around them. Laura clung to Chris's arm.

"Now this place is getting really spooky," she whimpered. "Chris, I want to go home."

"Shhh!" he cautioned, "be still." As though it were aflame, the air around them grew brighter. Then they heard a voice coming from behind them.

"Children. Do not be frightened."

The voice caused waves of goose pimples to spread over their bodies. They turned around to see who it was that was speaking to them. At first, they saw no one. Then, out of the glowing fog a lady appeared. She was the fairest lady they'd ever seen. Her flowing dress was sky blue, and on her head was a Christmas wreath with twelve burning candles. They looked at her with mouths agape and eyes wide with amazement.

"I'm here to guide and protect you," she said.

"Who are you?" Laura asked in her politest voice.

"You may call me Lady if you wish," the beautiful creature replied. "I am your friend, and I have come to lead you safely through the lands of Arboria. That is our name for this Christmas Tree World."

"We're very glad to see you," Laura said with such relief that tears came to her eyes. "This place is scary. That pig and dog just over the hill are fighting over apples. Can you tell us who they are?"

"Don't you recognize them?" Lady asked. "They were ornaments on your Christmas tree."

Laura thought for a moment. "Oh, yes, I remember now!" she exclaimed. "Those are Fat Pig and Old Mutt!"

"I beg your pardon," Lady replied.

"Aunt Pearl gave me Fat Pig, and Uncle Bert gave Chris Old Mutt," Laura explained. "Chris, you remember, don't you?"

"Sure," he replied. "But they're as big as we are. Have we shrunk?"

"One could say that," Lady said. "It all started happening the moment you placed the magic ornament on the tree. Your Christmas dream has begun."

"So Daddy was right after all!" exclaimed Laura. "His story about Gabriel's Magic Ornament is really true!"

"I know it's hard to believe," Lady said, "but yes. And soon you will begin your journey. But you must be brave and courageous. Only then will you see the evil in Arboria come to an end."

"Evil? Inside our Christmas tree?" asked Chris.

"Have you forgotten that all the lights on that bottom branch have burned out?" Lady asked him. "In Arboria, we call the Christmas lights 'angel stars'. They guide the people of Arboria and protect them from danger. But there is also a villain here called Lesnit. He eats angel stars because light is his favorite food. Most of all, Lesnit wants to eat the highest and brightest star, the star that burns above all Arboria. We call it the Star at Tree Top."

"That really is terrible," Laura remarked.

"Terrible hardly describes it," said Lady. "There are other grave problems here as well. Stoop down and feel the ground."

The children knelt down and felt of it. The ground was parched, and all the vegetation was dying.

"That, too, is Lesnit's doing. As he passes through Arboria, he sucks water from the tree branches. Arboria is drying up because of him. If it caught fire, he no doubt would be very happy."

"What makes him do such awful things?" Laura asked.

"Yeah," said Chris. "What does he have against our Christmas tree anyway?"

"You will find out in time," she replied. "Meanwhile, you must be very careful to stay out of his way. When you figure out where he is headed, just head in the opposite direction."

"Believe me, we will," Laura assured her.

"But how can we stay out of his way when we don't know what he looks like?" Chris asked.

"If I could describe him for you, I would," said Lady. "The problem is that he has many disguises and many faces. Some of his faces are pleasant. Others are so horrible you cannot bear to look upon them. Sometimes he wears beautiful masks, but you should always remember that under all his masks are hidden a very hideous face. He is the awful dragon of the night, a pitch-black serpent of darkness that comes from the wilderness beneath Arboria. The creature also has many names. 'Lesnit' is only one of them. His many disguises make it easy for him to creep through the branches of Arboria undetected, and because he's eaten so many angel stars, the Orna folk cannot reach Tree Top now."

"The Orna folk?" Laura inquired. "Who are they?"

"They are the people who dwell in Arboria," replied Lady. "In your world you knew them as the Christmas ornaments you used to decorate your tree. But here they are beautiful but fragile beings with thin skin and hollow hearts. Their hearts are empty and hopeless because Lesnit has ended their chances of escape from the lower branches of Arboria by blocking roads and destroying bridges that lead to Tree Top."

"There has to be some way to stop him," Chris blurted out with a frown. "If I see him, I'll beat his ugly head in."

"That would not stop him," Lady said. "If anything it would only make him grow stronger and fiercer."

"Then what can stop him?" asked Laura.

"Not what," Lady replied, "but who. Only a grandchild of Eva Isha Adams, the woman who originally let Lesnit out of a bag he was in, can stop him."

"Why did Eva 'what-cha-ma-call-it' do that?" Chris asked. "She must have been pretty dumb."

"Eva Isha Adams," Lady clarified. "I don't believe the poor thing realized what she'd done until it was too late. Have you ever heard the story of Pandora's box?"

"Oh, yeah," said Chris "I know that story from my book on Greek mythology. Pandora was told not to open a box, but she got curious and opened it anyway. When she did, all kinds of evil things escaped."

"That's right," Lady said. "She should have never let her curiosity cause her to lift the lid of that box. Curiosity got the better of Eva Isha Adams, too, because she couldn't wait until Christmas day to find out what was in the bag. She convinced her husband that it would be all right to peek, but when they did, they let Lesnit out. They did this despite the warnings of Tree King not to do it. I know that Eva and her husband wouldn't have done it if only they had known how bad things would get. They should have listened to Tree King."

Chris suddenly felt ashamed and nervous because he had carefully opened one of his presents under the tree, peeked to see what was inside, and flawlessly rewrapped it without his parents or anyone else knowing.

"Who is Tree King?" Laura asked Lady.

"He's the one who caused Arboria to grow from nothing. His dwelling is inside the star I told you about—the Star at Tree Top. Tree King is kind and good, but he is also very mysterious. No one has ever seen him or ever will. Not even I have seen him."

"Surely he will figure out a way to stop Lesnit," said Laura.

"If anyone can, Tree King can," Lady replied. "But the time has to be right, and the grandchild of Eva Isha Adams must be ready to assist when that time comes."

"I must leave you for now," said Lady. "But before I go, I must warn you about something else. If you get hungry, do not eat the apples here in Arboria."

"Why not? Is something wrong with them?" asked Chris.

"Yes, they are poisonous," Lady warned. "Every time Lesnit devours an angel star, he hiccups and an apple pops out of his mouth. They look delicious, but they never satisfy hunger the way apples normally do. If you eat one, you will only get hungrier and hungrier with each bite you take. You will want more and more of them, but they will never fill you up. Will you promise not to eat any?"

"We promise," the children assured her.

"One more thing," Lady warned. "Stay away from the mistletoe. It also is Lesnit's doing. Wherever he spits, mistletoe grows. While it is beautiful to look at, its white berries are deadly. Lesnit's mistletoe destroys the good things of Arboria. It offers nothing in return but harms whatever it touches. So beware its dark, magic spell." After these words, Lady turned and walked back into the swirling fog.

"Goodbye for now, children. You will see me again soon," they heard her say after she had disappeared, and the children wished her "goodbye."

"It was good meeting you," Laura added, waving a final goodbye as the fog slowly lifted.

— Chapter Two —

KNOWING A "BAD APPLE"
WHEN YOU SEE ONE

AFTER LADY LEFT THE CHILDREN, they saw Fat Pig and Old Mutt approaching. The flash of lightning followed by the glowing fog must have sparked their curiosity, so they were coming to investigate. As the ugly animals hurried down the road, they were still arguing fiercely.

"Oh, dear, they've seen us," Laura said. "Maybe we should make a run for it."

"I don't think we need to be afraid of them," said Chris. "Remember they are our Christmas ornaments, and we are the ones who put them on our tree."

Fat Pig arrived first, squealing as he approached, "Can you help us settle our dispute? I had ten apples in my basket before Old Mutt knocked it out of my hand. Before I could put all my apples back in my basket, Old Mutt snatched one. It's my apple, not his. Don't you agree?"

"Unfair, Fat Pig!" barked Old Mutt. "You had thirteen apples a couple of minutes ago and you stole at least three from my basket before I knocked yours out of that filthy cloven hoof of yours! Admit that you gobbled down three of them! I saw you do it with my very own eyes! Now you want more than your share! That makes you the greedy one!"

"Who knows how many apples you gobbled down before you got to my extra one," Fat Pig retorted. "Three? Four? Five? Ten?"

"You're wrong," growled Old Mutt. "Only FAT PIGS eat more than their fair share and you certainly are A VERY FAT PIG!"

"We'll see who the greedy one is, you mean, old scoundrel," Fat Pig oinked. "Why don't you share that extra apple with these children? That'll settle our disagreement once and for all."

"Not until you share one of your apples, you overstuffed swine," insisted Old Mutt.

"Not on your life," squealed Fat Pig. "You go first."

Chris interrupted them. "Wait a minute. We don't want your apples."

"Yeah," said Laura. "The apples are bad for you. Don't you know that?"

Fat Pig and Old Mutt stared at each other in disbelief.

"Are you crazy?" squealed Fat Pig with a scowl. "Where'd you get that idea?"

"From Lady," replied Chris.

"Lady, who?" woofed Old Mutt. "One of those snobs from Upper Arboria, no doubt. Sounds like something one of them would say."

"What in the world are you talking about?" asked Chris. "Where is Upper Arboria?"

"He doesn't know where Upper Arboria is?" Fat Pig mumbled to Old Mutt. "Who are you anyway?" he grunted at the children. "You don't look like Orna folk."

"We're not. We're children," Laura answered. "We came to Arboria with the help of a magic ornament—Gabriel's Magic Ornament."

"That's hard to believe," replied Fat Pig. "And if you are children as you claim, what can you possibly know about our apples?"

"They make you hungrier with each bite you eat, and they never fill you up," Laura said, trying to convince him.

"She's right," said Chris. "Lady warned us not to eat any."

"There he goes with that 'Lady' talk again," howled Old Mutt. "Who is this 'Lady' person? Did she give you her name?"

"No," replied Chris. "She just told us to call her Lady."

"Sounds fishy to me," barked Old Mutt. "Didn't your mother tell you never to talk to strangers?"

"Yes," started Chris, "but..."

"Enough!" squealed Fat Pig. "Why don't you ask the old scoundrel for an apple? I'm sure he'd be glad to share it."

"Don't volunteer my apple, you horrendous hog!" barked Old Mutt.

"Stingy wolf!" grunted Fat Pig.

"Very well," Old Mutt said, pretending to give in. He grasped the apple in his paw and held it out to Chris. "I would like you to have this," he said. "Don't think I'm doing this because of anything Fatty Pork-bottom here says. I'm offering it to you out of the goodness and generosity of my heart. Call it a Christmas present."

"That's thoughtful of you," said Chris. "But..."

"Take it," squealed Fat Pig. "Old Mutt is offering it."

"If they don't want it, they don't have to take it!" growled Old Mutt.

"Your offer is generous, really," said Chris. "It's just that..."

"TAKE THE THING!" Fat Pig insisted. "Can't you see it's the only way to end our quarrel?"

"All right," said Chris. "Thank you. I will use it as a Christmas ornament when I get home."

"WHAT!" Fat Pig oinked. "And waste a perfectly good apple? You either have to eat it or give it back this minute."

"He can't eat it, remember?" Laura warned. "Lady told us not to eat the apples, no matter how hungry we get."

"Then give it to me!" Fat Pig grunted, grabbing it out of Chris's hand and running away."

"Stop," Old Mutt yelped, chasing after him. "Come back with my apple!"

Old Mutt stayed hot on the trail of Fat Pig until they were out of sight.

"My, they're high strung," Laura remarked. "Could it have been the apples that made them so ornery?"

"That would explain a lot," Chris said. "Just think. If we hadn't met Lady, we might have eaten one of those apples without knowing how dangerous they are. I have a bad feeling the whole land of Lower Arboria is in trouble. The sad thing is that no one seems to know it. We'd better leave before Old Mutt and Fat Pig come back. Let's follow the road and see where it leads."

The children had traveled for about a mile when the road became blocked by a wall of mistletoe. It grew so thickly, they would have to cut through to go any further.

"This must be Lesnit's doing," said Chris. "If only we had some hedge clippers."

"I don't think there's any way across it," said Laura, standing on tiptoes. "Should we try to find a way around?"

A voice from behind them spoke. "There is no way around."

They turned and saw a very dirty snowman standing there with a sad look on his face.

"Believe me, I've tried to find one," Snowman said.

"Then you've tried to cut through it?" Chris asked.

"That wouldn't do any good. Beyond the mistletoe is a gigantic hole, so large and deep and dark, no one can get across it. If somebody were to fall into that hole, I shudder to think what might happen to him."

"How did the hole get there?" Chris asked.

"Once an angel star burned there, but when old Lesnit gobbled it up he left that hole behind. Deep inside it, an awful, hungry, dark fire now burns."

"You know about Lesnit?" Laura asked Snowman.

"Oh, yes. He's a dangerous one, he is. It's best to stay as far away from him as possible."

"Earlier, we met a pig and a dog fighting over one of Lesnit's apples," Chris told him.

"Yes," Laura chimed in. "They didn't seem to know who Lesnit was, and they did not know his apples were dangerous. A person called Lady warned us that the apples would make us hungrier and hungrier with each bite. We promised her we wouldn't eat any, no matter how hungry we got."

"Lady was right, and I'm so glad you listened to her," said Snowman. "The apples are bringing a terrible blight on our land. You must come with me to my igloo. I will tell you more about Lower Arboria and our apple problem. It's a very sad tale, I'm afraid."

Chris and Laura followed Snowman and soon were sitting on ice chairs at an ice table inside his igloo.

"Would you like a bowl of snowflakes to eat?" Snowman asked. "I'm sure you must be hungry."

"That's very kind of you," Laura replied politely. "But I think snowflakes might make us cold. Thank you anyway."

"I'm sorry I don't have other food to offer," said Snowman, taking off his spectacles and polishing them.

Putting them back on, he looked carefully at his guests. "I see now you are not Orna folk."

"No, we're children," said Chris. "We came here with the help of a magic ornament—Gabriel's Magic Ornament."

"Yes," said Laura. "When we met Lady, she told us about the evil serpent, Lesnit, who tries to destroy Arboria by eating the angel stars. Then we met Fat Pig and Old Mutt and figured out that what Lady had said must be the truth."

"Lady is very wise," said Snowman. "I was nearby when Lesnit came. With my own eyes I saw him gobble up an angel star. It was such a horrible sight. It causes me pain even to talk about it. The explosion Lesnit caused was more terrible than anything I've ever seen. That's how I got so dirty. I was too close to the explosion and got contaminated by the fallout. I'm afraid there's nothing I can do about it either."

"Couldn't you take a bath?" Chris suggested.

"My dear child," he chuckled. "I am a snowman. Can you imagine what would happen if I were to step in water? I would instantly lose a leg, or worse!"

"I see what you mean," Chris realized. "But there must be some way to clean you up. Maybe you could be dry-cleaned or something."

Snowman laughed. "I think not, dear boy. I fear I'm stuck in my present state until I melt."

"We're sorry," said Laura. "It must be very hard for you."

"You're considerate and kind to think about me," Snowman replied, "but there are Orna folk in Lower Arboria who are much worse off than I. I suppose by now you know there is no way out of this place."

"I don't guess we knew that," Chris said.

"You see," Snowman explained. "All Arboria was once connected by roads that were lit by angel stars. Now the bridges are out and all the roads are blocked. No one can leave."

"Why is that so bad?" asked Laura.

"You must understand that Orna folk can only become brighter and more beautiful the farther up the tree they travel. It's like going to school. Every Orna comes from the bottom of our Tree World. They are all born there. Then they journey upward, learning lessons and gaining knowledge. As they become wiser, they shine more and more brightly. Finally, when they are ready, they enter the glorious Star at Tree Top where Tree King dwells."

"Lady told us about Tree King," said Laura. "I hope we can meet him some day."

"Indeed, I would like very much to do so myself," said Snowman. "Of course you know that Orna folk cannot enter his palace until they are ready. They must first struggle upward through the branches, and that's not an easy thing. The journey through the branches is hard, causing many to try to look for a simpler way. That is so sad because it turns out that the easier way is no real way at all. It leads not to the top but to the bottom of our Tree World. The easy way that leads nowhere is always Lesnit's way.

"No, it's only by taking the hard road that the Orna folk are made to shine with greater and greater brightness until at last they enter into the Star at Tree Top. Now that the angel stars are being gobbled up by Lesnit, I'm afraid there's no way for the Orna to get to the next round of branches, much less to Tree Top. But there is another reason the Orna folk have given up."

"What reason is that?" asked Chris.

"They are addicted to Lesnit's apples," Snowman replied. "Lesnit not only gobbles up the lights that guide Orna folk out of their darkness, he feeds the Orna his apples to make their darkness grow ever deeper. That is why the Ornas, while beautiful on the outside, are hollow and hopeless on the inside. It's a terrible thing. The apples are Lesnit's substitutes for angel stars. The Orna folk eat them hoping that they will find an easy way out of Lower Arboria. But the apples lead only to the deep pits that Lesnit leaves behind whenever he devours an angel star. If someone eats Lesnit's apples, he will no longer want to go to the Star at Tree Top. Instead, he will gorge himself like Lesnit who gulps down everything that shines. Eventually, the Orna folk who eat the apples jump into the pits and end up falling into the horrible wilderness at Tree Bottom."

"Lady told us that eating Lesnit's apples makes a person's hunger grow worse and worse," said Laura. "But I don't understand how they lead to the deep pits?"

"I don't either," replied Snowman, "but I've seen it happen many times, and I'm sure if you stay here long enough you will see it, too. Even now, Lesnit crawls upward toward the higher branches of Arboria. The top branches will not fall under Lesnit's spell as quickly as the lower ones, but they will fall under his spell eventually if folks listen to him."

"I hope they're smart enough not to listen," said Chris. "Maybe when they hear about what's happened here in Lower Arboria, they'll send rescue squads."

"Yes," Laura added. "That would be wonderful."

"I'll believe that when I see it," said Snowman. "Meanwhile, Lower Arboria will suffer from Lesnit's evil deeds."

While they talked with Snowman in his igloo, they heard a terrible racket outside. They ran out the door and again saw Fat Pig and Old Mutt fighting. The animals had eaten all the apples they had gathered and struggled furiously to have the last one remaining.

"I don't think anybody can help them now," said Chris. "Just look at them. They can't see past their own selfishness for anything."

"They can't help themselves," Snowman sniffled. "Lesnit's hunger burns in them so fiercely, they can't rest. They're so addicted to his apples that it's only a matter of time before they are devoured by their own hunger."

"I can't bear to watch anymore," said Laura, covering her eyes.

Just then Old Mutt chased Fat Pig toward the mistletoe.

"Stop!" shouted Chris. "Stop or you'll die!"

Fat Pig and Old Mutt didn't listen. They just ran right over the mistletoe into the pit Lesnit had made. Chris and Laura could hear them squealing and yelping as they fell in.

"That's the end of them," said Snowman with a look of sadness. "That hole is one of Lesnit's many mouths. He has eaten those poor creatures alive. Now they'll just be more fuel for his deep, dark, hungry fire."

Chris and Laura stood quietly, looking toward the place where Fat Pig and Old Mutt had disappeared. There was only silence. Lesnit had done his awful work. His victims were cantankerous, true, but they surely didn't deserve to come to such a horrible end.

The children had been standing by Snowman for some time, sad and silent, when a ring of twelve stars formed in the sky above the pit. The ring moved towards them until its stars miraculously changed into the flames of Lady's crown and she once again appeared to them.

"This part of your journey is over," she told the children. "I'm sorry you had to see that sad sight, but I thought you needed to witness first hand some of the horrible happenings inside our beautiful Tree World. I'm sorry to tell you that further disturbing episodes lie ahead. However, if you are to join us in our efforts to overcome Lesnit's evil spell, I must do what I can to show you what Lesnit is up to. It's time now children to fly to the next round of branches and see what awaits us there. Are you ready to go?"

"Oh, please," said Laura. "Can we take Mr. Snowman with us? He's been so kind. We can't just leave him here."

"Snowman may come if he wishes," said Lady. "But his help is needed more here in Lower Arboria. It might be better if he stayed and gave a hand to those who desperately need him."

"Lady is right," agreed Snowman. "I must stay here and do what I can to save the Orna folk from their apple addiction."

"I'm glad we met you," said Chris. "Maybe we'll see you again later."

"Yes," added Laura. "We'll try to come back and see you. I know that soon you will be sparkling clean again because you have such a good heart."

"Thank you, kind children," replied Snowman. "Good bye for now. And be careful on your journey."

"It's time, children," said Lady. "Join hands with me."

As they all three held each other's hands, they were magically transported over the pit of endless darkness. They could almost feel the pit pulling them toward it like a magnet, and they were very grateful for Lady's protection. Soon, they found themselves on the next round of branches. When they looked around for Lady, she had vanished again. She had left them on a sidewalk surrounded by somewhat tarnished Orna folk.

—Chapter Three—

MAIDS A MILKING, LORDS A LEAPING, AND BIRDS OF A FEATHER

CARS, TAXIS, AND BUSES, bumper to bumper, inched their way down the busy street. Drivers slammed brakes, honked horns, and shouted rude words. "Move!" yelled a newspaper boy as he whizzed past an old lady walking down the sidewalk. She stumbled and tried to slam him with her purse. "Silly little fool!" she yelled. "Doesn't your mother teach you anything?"

Orna folk crowded the streets, rushed in and out of stores, and glanced at long shopping lists. Everybody ignored a choir singing Christmas carols. As one man shoved past, Chris tried to stop him. "Sir, can you tell us where we are?" He paid Chris no mind but just glared at his wristwatch.

"Everybody here seems to have a one-track mind," Laura stated.

"They're rude, if you ask me," said Chris. "Let's try that store over there."

The store was called Partridges and Pears, and inside a mob pushed to buy sale items. The children found a saleslady in a pink pinafore. She was trying to sell an expensive porcelain bird figurine to a customer.

"Excuse me," Chris interrupted. "Can you help us?"

The saleslady glared at him. "Can't you see I'm busy?"

An announcement blared over the loud speakers, "Attention, shoppers! Golden rings now on sale! Get them while they last!"

"Golden rings!" exclaimed the saleslady's customer. "Just what I need!" And off she sped.

"I hope you children are happy. I lost that sale, thanks to you," the saleslady said as she yanked a huge purse from under the shelf, dug through it, pulled out a mirror and lipstick, and smeared some on her mouth. Laura noticed that her nametag read: "Mrs. E. Adams, MILKMAID."

Just then, a floor manager came bouncing toward them, and Mrs. Adams jumped in front of him and shouted, "Sir!"

"Lords a leaping, woman! I almost ran you down!"

"These children are not with their parents and seem to be lost," Mrs. Adams said. "I don't have time to mess with them."

"Can't you brats ever stay with your mommies?" the manager growled. "What am I supposed to do about them?"

Before Mrs. Adams could answer, he ordered, "Take them to Lost and Found," and bounced away.

"Adams," Laura whispered to Chris. "Isn't she the one who let Lesnit out of the bag?"

"Are you by chance Eva Isha Adams?" Laura asked the saleslady.

"Heavens, no," she replied as she grabbed their arms and led them through the crowd. "I've never heard of anyone by that name. My name is Elvira Adams."

"Why does your tag say Milkmaid?" asked Chris. "Are there cows here?"

"Silly boy. What kind of a milkmaid do you think I am?"

"I don't know. What kind are you?" Chris replied.

The woman looked around to see if anyone was listening, and then whispered in his ear. "We 'milk' customers!" Chris could smell a hint of apple cider vinegar on her warm breath. Or was it her thick lipstick?

Laura looked puzzled.

"You don't get it, do you?" whispered Mrs. Adams. "We 'milk' customers for 'moola'. We charge them as much money as they will pay." She chuckled. "They think a sale is always going on. Today is our Red Apple sale."

The children's jaws dropped.

"That doesn't seem like a very good way to advertise," said Chris. "Don't you know the apples here are dangerous?"

Mrs. Adams cackled. "You have a cute sense of humor, young man. Now, here is Lost and Found. Give the clerk your names. If you're lucky, they'll locate your parents."

"But our parents are not..." Chris began, but Mrs. Adams interrupted him with a "shush" and told them she had to get back to her sales counter.

At a desk sat a clerk wearing a crownless cap. He was writing and didn't bother to look up. "If you've lost something, don't tell me. Everything has been claimed."

"We're here because Mrs. Adams thinks we're lost," said Chris.

The clerk looked up. "Lost? That figures. Your parents must not care about you. Never mind. We have entertainment just beyond those doors." He pointed. "You can stay until your parents come—if they ever do come. Most of them don't, you know."

Chris wanted to explain to the clerk that they knew where their parents were and that they were not really lost. However, all he could get out were the words "But we're not..." before the clerk interrupted him with a loud "GO ALONG NOW! CAN'T YOU SEE I'M BUSY? THE DOORS ARE THERE!" and he pointed again to show them the way without looking up from what he was doing.

"Gosh," Laura said to her brother as they entered a hallway that looked like the entrance to a cinema, "it's sure hard to get anybody to pay attention here." They could hear loud music blaring behind some doors.

"Never mind," Chris said as he headed to the doors. "Let's see what's going on inside here."

When they walked through the door, they saw hundreds of children watching a show. Ladies danced on the stage, and drummers and pipers pounded and squealed out deafening punk rock music. Everyone seemed to be having a great time.

"I don't feel good about this," said Laura. "Those dancing ladies don't look very nice. And listen to that music. Do you think Mom and Dad would approve?"

"Aw, don't be such a spoiled sport," said Chris. "It won't hurt to watch one show, will it? Anyway, my feet are really starting to hurt."

Chris and Laura took their seats and soon were clapping to the music. A little while later, a vendor came prancing down the isle, passing out candy apples. "Here kids, these're on the house," and he tossed a couple to Chris and Laura.

Without thinking, Chris started to bite into it, but Laura quickly jerked it away from his mouth before he could do it. "What is wrong with you?" she yelled. "They're apples. Remember?"

"Surely one little bite won't hurt," Chris said. "I'm so hungry."

"Earth to Chris," Laura said with a stare. "Don't you remember what Lady said? That apple will make you hungrier with each bite you eat!"

"Oh, alright, don't be such a worry wart!" he said, wrapping the apple in his napkin and setting it on the floor.

"Do you know what I'm thinking?" Laura asked. "I'm thinking the music and dancing are fogging our minds. What if those are pied pipers up there playing—the kind that lead children astray? I think we'd better leave while we still can."

"Maybe you're right," Chris agreed, so they got up, left the theater, and returned to the mall. As they walked along, they saw more children watching television and playing video games. Just then, a boy leaving an arcade noticed Chris and Laura.

"Hi," he greeted them. "Are you new here?"

"I guess so," Chris answered.

"I'm going to the carnival," the boy said. "Want to come along?"

"Sure, that sounds like fun," Chris answered. Then he asked his sister. "Do you want to go?"

"I guess so," she replied. "I just hope they don't try to give us any of those horrible apples."

"How long have you been here?" the boy asked.

"Oh, only thirty minutes or so," Chris said.

"Is that all? Then you haven't had time to do much of anything, have you?"

"I guess not."

"Come with me. I know everything there is to do here."

"How long have you been lost?" Laura asked the boy.

"Two days."

"That's too bad," said Laura. "Are you worried that your parents won't come?

"Are you kidding?" the boy asked, chuckling. "Parents are a problem if you ask me. They tell you what to do and what not to do. But nothing like that spoils your fun here. You don't have to do homework. You don't have to go to bed when you're told. You don't have to do anything you don't want to do. I don't care if my parents never show up."

"Surely you miss them," Laura suggested.

"Are you crazy? Of course I don't miss them. I'm having the time of my life."

"But your parents must miss you. Think of how worried they must be."

"Believe me. They're glad to get me out of their hair. They don't care a lick where I am. They're too busy with their parties and stuff. They've never had time for me anyway. Come on, and I'll show you some cool stuff."

Chris and Laura could hear carnival music and laughter.

"Over here," said the boy. "The roller coaster ride is this way. I haven't tried it yet, but I hear it's great. You've got to ride it with me."

Hundreds of children were on the many rides, eating candy apples, and having great fun. The only adults around were those operating rides, but they seemed more like robots than people.

"This is not good," Laura whispered to Chris. "See? There are the candy apples again. And look at those people operating the rides. They look like escaped convicts."

"Laura, try not to say anything, okay?" Chris requested. "You will embarrass us."

"This is it," said the boy as they arrived at the roller coaster ride. "The line's long, but I hear the ride is worth the wait."

A girl in the line took a candy apple from her purse and munched on it. Laura and Chris glanced at each other nervously.

"I hope you know those apples are bad for you," Laura whispered to the girl.

The girl laughed and shouted out so that everyone could hear, "Who are you, my mommy or something?" The others in the line around them laughed, too, and Laura turned so red from embarrassment that her head looked like one of the candy apples.

"What is this ride called?" Chris asked.

"The Dragon's Den," said the boy. "Isn't that cool?"

Laura noticed some shrubbery near the ride's entrance and whispered in her brother's ear, "Is that mistletoe?"

"Nah, I don't think so," he whispered back.

Meanwhile, the vendor was crying out, "Candy apples! Get your candy apples!" Chris and Laura each took one but didn't eat it.

"What's wrong?" the boy probed. "Don't you like them?"

"Not really," said Chris. "I'm not much of an apple fan."

The boy laughed. "You goon! The apples are the best things here. You should at least try one."

Soon they saw the Dragon's Den sign at the coaster entrance. They could hear children on the ride screaming.

"I can't wait, can you?" said the boy. "This is going to be so much fun."

Laura glanced at the shrubbery again. This time she saw little white berries. Now there was no doubt the shrubbery was mistletoe, the work of Lesnit.

"I'm afraid, Chris," Laura whispered. "I have a very bad feeling about getting on that ride."

"I'll go alone, then," Chris told her. "You can wait for me at the exit."

"That won't work," said the boy overhearing. "The exit is outside the park. Once you ride the roller coaster, you're out for good. That's why I've waited until now. I'm bored, so I might as well go ahead and take my final fling."

"Then I guess you'll have to take it by yourself," said Chris. "I can't very well leave my sister behind."

"Let's go, Chris," said Laura. "I don't like this place."

As they hurried away from the line, the other children ridiculed them and called them names. This only made Chris and Laura hurry all the more. They soon found their way back to Lost and Found, but when they tried to leave, the clerk jumped up. "Where do you think you're going? You can't just leave. Your parents haven't come."

"This is a bad place," Chris told him. "We're out of here."

The clerk pushed a button, and seven floor managers immediately leapt through the door.

"These children are trying to escape," the clerk told them.

"We can't allow that now, can we?" a floor manager said. "We must meet our quota. I'm sorry, but you can't leave until your parents show up." His words brought an evil grin to the clerk's face.

At that moment, the door flew open, and a woman dressed in a blue suit and wearing a glittering Christmas hat walked in. "Children! There you are," she said. Chris and Laura were immensely relieved and so glad that Lady had come to their rescue.

"Wait just one minute," said the floor manager. "You know the rules. No child who has eaten an apple can leave."

"Yes," Lady said. "I know the rules. Children, did you keep your promise not to eat the apples?"

"Yes," they said.

"We didn't eat any of your apples," Laura added. "We swear we didn't."

"We'll just see about that," said the clerk as he took two apples out of his desk drawer. "Any child who has eaten one won't be able to resist another."

"No," refused Chris. "We don't want your apples. We know they're from your mean old hiccupping dragon."

The clerk looked shocked. Now their store wouldn't be able to meet its quota.

The children followed Lady back into the main part of the store. On their way out, they happened to pass by the toy department where a milkmaid was stocking a shelf with new dolls. When Laura recognized one, a look of horror came over her face.

"Look, Chris. That doll looks like that boy we met."

Chris stared. Next to it was another doll that looked like the girl who also had been in the roller coaster line. "You're right," he said to her. "They're all here."

"Can you believe it?" Laura asked Lady. "They're turning children into dolls! Can't something be done?"

"There is still hope for them," Lady answered. "If the dolls are loved, they could become human again. But it will take special children who will love them enough to make that happen."

"Please," said Laura, "may we buy the boy doll? He was a friend. I hate to think what might happen to him."

"Very well," agreed Lady. "But remember. He is very expensive, so you must take good care of him."

"I will," said Laura. "I promise I will."

After Lady paid for the doll, they left the store and soon were sailing with her through the air. Below they could see the amusement park. In its center was one of the large, gaping holes Lesnit had left behind when he had devoured an angel star. Lady's appearance had now changed. She again wore her flowing blue dress and the Christmas wreath with twelve candles the children had seen her in earlier. Soon, they were entering another part of Arboria.

—Chapter Four—

THE PRICE AT WHICH
YOU EAT SUGAR!

WHEN LADY VANISHED AGAIN, the children found themselves on Christmas Candy Way. Wrought iron street lamps lined the avenue, and strung from them were Christmas lights nestled in golden tinsel and shining like bright stars. Quaint candy shops and bakeries were decked out with boughs of holly and evergreen. Wonderful odors wafted on the air—cinnamon and gingerbread, fresh-baked pastries, chocolate and maple fudge, peppermint and roasted nuts. Through frosted windows, Chris and Laura could see shopkeepers dressed in colorful Christmas clothes. As they entered a shop, an old Orna woman greeted them. She wore a green satin dress, a lace blouse, and a vest made of red velvet. Her silver hair was pulled into a bun, and she smiled like one of the pudgy angels on Chris and Laura's Christmas tree.

"Hello, children," the old woman greeted them. "I'm Granny Applegate, but all the kids call me Granny A. May I help you?"

"We're starved," said Chris. "Apples are everywhere, but we can't eat them."

"Well, dear boy, you've come to the right place," she said. "We have all kinds of goodies—candy, cookies, gingerbread, nuts. What would you like?"

Laura kept eyeing a mountain of chocolate fudge behind the glass window. She had a sweet tooth, and there were many kinds of candy to choose from. "May I have some of that fudge?" she asked. "And some sugar cookies and peppermint candy, too?"

"Of course, you sweet little thing, you can have anything your heart desires." Then Granny A. smiled at Chris. "What will you have, dear boy?"

"I'd like that gingerbread. Do you have any cashew nuts?"

"Indeed, we do."

"Do you have pistachios?" Laura asked.

"Of course." Granny A. filled one bag with candy, another with gingerbread and cookies, and two others each with cashew and pistachio nuts. "Here, my dears. Over there are tables and chairs. Would you like sodas? We have lime fizzy water here."

"That sounds scrumptious," said Laura.

"Oh, it is to die for," Granny A. said, smiling. "Take your goodies to one of those tables over there, and enjoy yourselves."

"Thank you," said Laura. "You're the nicest person we've met so far in Arboria."

The children went to a table and sat down. Laura whispered to Chris, "Isn't she nice? I can't believe we've finally found a friendly person here. She really seems to love children."

Chris took a bite of the gingerbread. "Wow, taste this. It's the best gingerbread I've ever eaten."

Laura nibbled at a piece. "You're right. That is good."

As they feasted on their gingerbread, cookies, nuts, and candy, they noticed a very fat girl and a very fat boy at the counter buying ten bags full of goodies each. They waddled over and sat at a table next to Chris and Laura.

"Hello," the boy said. "I'm Jimmy."

"Hi. I'm Chris, and this is Laura."

"This is my sister, Sally," said Jimmy.

"Hi, Sally," the children said.

"Have you eaten any gingerbread yet?" Jimmy asked.

"Yes," Chris replied. "It's the best."

"Well...there's a place down the street where it's even better," Jimmy said. "This is the best place for candy, though," he added.

Chris noticed, however, that Jimmy was chomping on gingerbread and asked, "Why are you eating gingerbread here then?"

"Because this is candy day, and the store with the best gingerbread is too far down the street for me to waste time and energy going there. I don't want to tire myself out when there are more important things to do," Jimmy replied.

"Like what?" Chris asked.

"Like eating, of course. Can't you see how much I have to eat today? I'll never get it all down if I waste time walking to the other gingerbread store."

"Oh," replied Chris.

"Well, it's been good talking to you," said Jimmy. "I'm sorry, but I have a tight schedule to keep and must start eating now."

Jimmy and Sally proceeded to gorge themselves with candy, cakes, cookies, nuts, and pastries. They seemed to swallow everything whole, and as they did, they grew larger and larger before Chris's and Laura's very eyes. Before long, Granny A. returned.

"Ready for more goodies?" she asked Chris and Laura.

"No, thanks," Chris replied. "I'm full."

"Me, too," added Laura.

"You must be ready for your check then," said Granny A. "I'll bring it."

Chris and Laura stared at each other. Check? How would they pay? They had no money.

"Boy did you make a mistake," fat Sally said between bites. "Don't you know that you are safe only as long as you keep on eating?"

"Safe from what?" asked Laura.

"Just wait until you get the bill," said Sally. "You'll see."

Soon Granny A. returned. The check was for twenty five dollars and fifty-three cents.

"This has got to be wrong!" exclaimed Chris.

"I'm sorry," said Granny A. "Maybe I didn't figure it right."

She left for a moment and soon returned. "You are right, my dear. I'm so sorry I made a mistake in my addition. The bill is for thirty five dollars and fifty-three cents."

"I don't understand," Chris said nervously. "There is no way we can pay that much."

"Would you like me to put you on our delayed-payment plan?" Granny A. asked.

"What's that?" asked Chris.

"If you promise to come at least once a week and eat from our special menu, you can keep coming without paying as long as you wish."

"What is your special menu?" asked Laura.

"Jimmy and Sally are eating from it today," said Granny A. "They'll have to eat it all before they qualify for delayed payment. Thus far, they've been among our best customers."

"What happens if you don't pay?" asked Chris.

"I would hate to see anything bad happen to you," said Granny A. "So, I think a delayed-payment plan is just what you need."

"All right," Chris said. "I guess we'll give it a try."

"Good," said Granny A. "I don't think you'll be sorry. All you need to do is just sign your names right next to this 'X'. Then we'll see you back here again next week."

Chris and Laura signed their names without reading the paper because the words were unfamiliar, the sentences were complicated, and the print was very small.

"That was smart," said Jimmy. "You really don't want to know what they do to children who don't pay their bills. As long as you keep eating, you'll be okay. Trust me."

Chris and Laura watched Jimmy and Sally as they gorged on more and more goodies. How could they eat so much without getting sick? Chris asked how they managed it.

"We've found a secret," said Jimmy. "We discovered something that makes you so hungry you can eat a horse. The best thing is that it's free, so you don't need to worry about running out."

"What is it?" asked Chris.

"Apples," Jimmy whispered. "They are great because they make you hungry enough to eat everything on the menu. I ate twelve apples this morning. If I wanted, I could eat this shop out of business without blinking an eye. All I have to do is eat a couple more apples."

Laura had a horrified look on her face. "Don't you know those apples are bad for you?" she warned. "They are Lesnit's apples. They're poisonous."

"Where did you get that dumb idea?" Fat Sally asked with a grin. "Eating the apples is the only way you can stay on the delayed-payment plan. Do you think you'd be able to eat all these goodies without them?"

Chris and Laura sat at the table with a look of worry plastered across their faces. They watched Jimmy and Sally eat and eat. Finally the two finished and arose to leave.

"Good bye," said Jimmy. "You want to know more about the apples? Come to the gingerbread store at the end of this street tomorrow. I'll tell you where to get them."

"Thanks," said Chris.

Jimmy and Sally had no sooner waddled out the door when Chris and Laura heard a loud explosion. They jumped up and looked out the window. In the pavement outside were two large, gaping holes. They ran out, followed by Granny A. and the shopkeepers.

"What happened to Jimmy and Sally?" Chris shouted.

"Sad, isn't it?" said Granny A. calmly. "I guess they ate so many goodies they popped."

Chris looked into the hole. Everything was black. There seemed to be no bottom to it.

"How sad it is when children eat too much candy and cookies," Granny A. said. "They shouldn't have eaten so much."

"Then why did you keep on feeding them?" Laura cried.

"It was their choice, my dear. They could have paid their bill at any time, but instead they signed up for our delayed-payment plan, just as you did."

"We don't want to end up like Jimmy and Sally," said Laura. "I don't want to be part of your delayed-payment plan if this is going to happen to us."

"Very well," said Granny A. "I'll get your bill."

"But we can't pay it!" exclaimed Chris. "What'll we do?"

"Follow me," said Granny A. "I'll explain our terms."

They followed her into the store. Fear gnawed at their stomachs as she did some figuring on the bill and then handed it to Chris. When he read it, his eyes bugged out.

"Six trillion, nine-hundred-fifty million dollars?" Chris cried. "Our bill is trillions of times more than it should be."

"Maybe you didn't read the fine print on the paper you signed," replied Granny A. "You agreed to pay your own debt, plus the debt of all the children who have exploded, plus interest. Jimmy and Sally had a very large bill, not to mention the many other children who've exploded. Now you'll have to pay all the costs."

"That's unfair," Laura argued.

"I'm sorry, dear," said Granny A., "but you did sign your names."

Laura started weeping, and Chris fought back tears. He tried to act brave, but he was truly scared.

"Don't cry, my dears," Granny A. said. "We have another plan. We have a work farm for children. I'm sure you'll be able to pay off your debt in time."

"Alright," said Chris. "What do we do?"

"Stay here. Mr. Budgens is our budget-balancer. He'll set up your new payment plan. Have a seat. He'll be with you shortly."

The seats were uncomfortable—hard and splintery.

Thirty minutes later, an old man entered the store. "Where are the delinquent customers?" he asked gruffly.

"Children," Granny A. said, "this is Mr. Budgens."

"Come into my office," he said.

They followed him to a room furnished with beautiful plush carpeting and soft armchairs. The children started to sit in the comfortable chairs.

"Not there, THERE!" growled Mr. Budgens, pointing to some hard, splintery benches. Suddenly, he spied the doll in Laura's arms. "What's that you're holding?"

"A doll. Lady bought it for me."

"Pretty expensive, too, by the look of it," said Mr. Budgens. "If we can sell it, I'll apply a portion of the money to your bill."

"Oh, please," begged Laura. "Don't take him away."

"GIVE IT HERE!" shouted Mr. Budgens. "Where you're going, there will be no time to play with dolls."

Laura began to whimper.

"Now," said Mr. Budgens, looking over the signed paper. "It says here you agreed to pay six trillion, nine-hundred-fifty million dollars. You say you don't have the money. You should be ashamed coming in here and eating our goodies when you don't have money to pay for them. Shame, shame on you!"

"We're sorry," said Chris. "We didn't know."

"YOU DIDN'T KNOW!" shouted Mr. Budgens. "That's what they all say. Well you know now, don't you?"

"Yes," said Chris trembling. Laura started sobbing.

"You might as well stop that, young lady," barked Mr. Budgens. "It's not going to help you pay this debt."

"But can't we just forget it?" asked Chris. "Write it off as a mistake?"

"FORGET IT?" screamed Mr. Budgens. "We're not made of money, you know. We've got employees to pay. No, we can't just FORGET IT." Mr. Budgens started writing something on paper. Then he abruptly handed a copy to Chris and Laura.

"This is your new contract. Read over it."

Chris read carefully through teary eyes, but he choked when he saw these words: "Until my debt is paid in full, I agree to work for Budgens Enterprises as a farm laborer at the rate of ten cents per day. I understand that I will have to work whether I'm sick or not."

"I can't sign this," said Chris. "We'll never pay off the debt if we make only ten cents a day."

"That's too bad, isn't it?" said Mr. Budgens. "I'm afraid you have no other choice now. You've made your mistake."

"And what if I don't sign it?" Chris asked him.

"We'll put you in prison, and you'll be forced to labor. That will be even worse than the farms."

A sad look came over Chris and Laura's faces. They had no other option. They soon boarded a hay wagon to one of the farms.

"I can't believe that Mr. Budgens is so mean," Chris said. "We weren't even given a choice. We had to sign those papers."

"I know," said Laura. "What will we do?"

"I'm not sure," whispered Chris. "Maybe we can run away."

When the children arrived at the work farm, guards opened the gates. Ahead they could see ugly, run-down buildings with paint peeling off their rotten boards.

"Those will be your quarters," said the driver harshly. "And by the way, I heard you whisper earlier that you and your sister might try to escape. Don't even think about it. They have dogs here—big ones the size of horses—and mean, too. They'll sic 'em on you if you try anything stupid. Now get out. It's time you reported to Mrs. Margumont. She's in that building. Hurry or she'll scold you for being late."

The children jumped off the hay wagon. When they entered the building, they saw a large, very ugly woman with stringy, oily hair sitting at a desk. Frowning, she stood and yelled, "What are you children doing in here? Don't you have the decency to knock?"

"We're sorry," said Chris, taking several steps back.

"I'll pardon you this once," Mrs. Margumont grumbled. "But you had better not make any more mistakes. Is that clear?"

"Yes, ma'am," said Chris.

Mrs. Margumont stared at Laura. "I'm talking to you, too, young lady."

"Yes, ma'am," Laura answered, trying to hold back tears.

"There are work clothes in that room. Change into them, and I'll tell you what we expect from our workers. Now hurry. We don't waste time here."

In a few moments, Chris and Laura returned dressed in their work clothes.

"You're going to have to change faster than that in the future," said Mrs. Margumont. "Here's the schedule. You will report to the mess hall at six in the morning. You've got five minutes to eat breakfast. At six-o-five you'll be in the sugar cane fields or we'll deduct from your pay. You will harvest cane until one o'clock. Then you'll have five minutes for lunch before returning to the fields at one-o-five. Quitting time is seven o'clock. And don't try to quit early, or you'll have to work in the fields until ten. There's nothing worse than working in a dark sugarcane field, so don't try anything silly. The quota is twelve wagonloads of sugarcane per person per day. Do you children know what a quota is?"

"No, ma'am," they replied.

"A quota means you have to fill twelve wagons and no less. Do you understand what I'm saying?"

"Yes, ma'am."

"Good. Now I'll make a deal with you. If you can fill fifteen wagons a day for a month, I'll promote you to the presses. The work's hard there, too, but not as hard as the fields. Now it's two o'clock. I still expect each of you to fill your daily quota. That's twelve wagonloads each, remember. If you don't fill them all, they will be added to tomorrow's quota. Is that clear?"

"Yes, ma'am," replied Chris and Laura.

"Very well." Mrs. Margumont blew her whistle, and a guard entered. "Take these urchins to the fields and make them work."

The guard gave the children dull machetes to cut the cane. In the fields, children were everywhere working hard and fast to fill wagons.

"Your wagons are there," the guard pointed. "Now get busy."

Chris and Laura started cutting cane and filling wagons.

"I'll bet they use this cane to make sugar for the candy we ate earlier," said Chris

"How are we ever going to fill these wagons?"

"We had better get to work, or we won't," said Chris. "Who knows what will happen if we don't fill them."

The children worked hard, and the hours passed slowly. At long last, seven o'clock came, but Chris and Laura had filled only one wagon with cane. The guards had taken their watches, so they didn't know what the time was until the whistle blew.

"That can't be the quitting whistle," Chris said in a panic.

"What will we do?" cried Laura.

"We've got to try to escape," replied Chris.

"Is that a good idea?" said Laura. "Those dogs might eat us alive."

"What other choice do we have?" Chris asked.

Soon the guard returned to check the children's work. Several had managed somehow to fill their twelve wagons. When the guard came to Chris and Laura though, he started shouting, "ONE WAGON? You lazy do-nothings, you are going to be sorry. I'm taking you to Mrs. Margumont."

When they arrived to see Mrs. Margumont, she was sitting behind her desk, eating a big plate of spaghetti and meatballs. Tomato sauce covered her chin and cheeks.

"What's the problem?" she said with a string of spaghetti plastered across her chin. "Is it important enough that my dinner be interrupted?"

"Yes, ma'am," said the guard. "These goof-offs filled only one wagon."

"One?" she whispered. Then she screamed "ONE! You children are going to be sorry you didn't work harder. Take these urchins back to the fields. There won't be any pay for you today. Not a penny."

"Please, ma'am," said Chris. "We're very hungry, and that spaghetti looks good. Could we...?"

"IMPUDENT BOY!" shouted Mrs. Margumont. "We don't serve this kind of food to children. You've got to pay for your own food, and you haven't made any money yet."

"Please," asked Laura, "couldn't we eat now and pay later?"

"We don't do that here," replied the ugly woman. "You'll have to go without tonight. Maybe you will have enough for dinner by tomorrow evening. Meals are ten cents each."

"Ten cents?" cried Chris. "That's what we make in a day! How do you expect us to live without food?"

"That's your problem, isn't it?" Mrs. Margumont spat. "And you'd better not use that tone of voice with me again, young man, or I'll send you straight to prison."

How could prison be any worse? Chris thought. The guard took them back to the fields. They were dark—too dark to work in—but Chris and Laura did the best they could.

Laura started sobbing. "I can't lift another finger. I'm so tired and hungry. I wish I were home with Mom and Dad. I wish Dad hadn't bought that stupid ornament. I think it was cursed."

"I do, too," said Chris. "It seems we're stuck in Arboria, and I don't have any idea how we're going to get home. We can't stay in this place, Laura. We've got to get out of here before the guard returns. Maybe we can run far enough away before they miss us. Come on."

"What about the terrible dogs?" Laura asked with panic in her voice.

"We'll just have to take our chances," Chris replied.

The children took off across the fields, running as fast as they could. It wasn't long before they came to a fence.

"We'd better test this to be sure it's not electric," Chris said, sticking out his hand and quickly touching the fence. "It's all right," he said. "Quick! Start climbing!"

Chris and Laura climbed over the fence and headed across a meadow. Laura finally collapsed. "It's no use. I can't go on."

"You don't have a choice!" Chris shouted. "They'll be looking for us!"

"Please, let me rest for just a few minutes."

Before a minute was up, they heard noises in the distance.

"Dogs!" Chris exclaimed, jumping up.

"Oh, no," cried Laura. "What'll we do now?"

"Run like you've never run before," Chris told her.

They ran so hard their lungs burned, but the barking got louder and louder. Soon they stumbled and fell on their faces.

"We're going to be eaten by dogs!" Laura cried.

They could not see well, but they knew they'd run into bushes.

"Gosh, look how thick these are. I wish I'd brought that machete," Chris said.

"Chris, it's mistletoe! Lesnit's mistletoe! You know what that means! One of those bottomless pits will be on the other side! We can't go this way!"

The barking got louder and louder. The children now could see lanterns swinging in the distance, and they could hear shouting. At that very instant they saw something so horrible they were almost paralyzed. The guards were riding dogs as big as horses!

"If we ever needed Lady, it's now," said Laura. "Please, Lady," she called. "Help us. Help us. Please."

The search party closed in. "They couldn't have gotten much further!" the children heard someone shout. "The mistletoe hedge is straight ahead! Nobody gets past that!"

"Chris, I'm so afraid," Laura whispered, holding on to him as they sat huddled at the foot of the mistletoe hedge.

The search party was less than fifty yards away now. The children knew their fate was sealed. Now it was only a matter of time before they were captured. As they sat there, trembling and waiting for the guards to come, suddenly, without warning, a pillar of fire sprang up between them and the approaching guards.

"Could that be Lesnit's fire?" asked Laura.

"No!" Chris shouted. "It's Lady! She's come to rescue us. Thank you, Lady!" The children started jumping up and down and shouting, "Yeah!"

Lady emerged from the fire, calm and serene, and said, "You are safe now. Come with me."

They followed her, and she lifted them up from the ground in the pillar of fire, across the mistletoe hedge, and over Lesnit's bottomless pit.

"You are hungry," Lady observed. "I have something for you." She gave them wafers of sweet bread. It was the most wonderful food the children had ever eaten. Then Lady allowed a deep sleep to come over them so they could rest. When the children awoke, Lady was still with them.

"Where are we now?" asked Chris, rubbing his eyes.

"Still hovering," replied Lady. "You must decide whether or not you want to go to the next land. Do you wish to go on?"

"I don't think so," sighed Laura. "I'm ready to go home. I want my parents."

Lady looked at Chris.

"Me, too," he said. "I've had enough excitement to last forever. I promise I'll never complain again about being bored."

"I will make it possible for you to return, then," said Lady. "But if you go back now, you will never return to Arboria, and you will never know how the dream ends. You should know that the best part of the dream is yet to come. Remember, I have promised to protect you. I will let no harm come to you."

Chris and Laura looked at one another. "What do you think? Do you want to stay?" Chris asked Laura.

"It's a hard decision." Laura thought for a minute. "I guess so."

"Then we'll stay," said Chris.

"You will not be sorry," said Lady. She waved her hands before her, and soon they were landing.

—Chapter Five—

ONE TIN SOLDIER RIDES AWAY

WHEN LADY VANISHED, the children stood in a strangely quiet and still wood. Not a bird chirped, and not a leaf rustled. The calm was eerie, like that in the eye of a hurricane.

"It may be my imagination," Chris whispered, "but I have the feeling somebody's watching us."

Laura looked around. "This place is spooky. Now I wonder whether Lady was telling us the truth about our dream getting better. After our experience with Granny Applegate, I'm not sure what to believe anymore."

The echo of a gunshot broke the silence. "That's not a good sign!" Chris exclaimed. "Let's get out of here!" He grabbed Laura by the hand, and they started to make a run for it.

"Are they shooting at us?" Laura cried.

"They may just be hunters," Chris replied. "If they are, we certainly don't want to get in their way. Look, there's a clearing ahead."

In the clearing was a cabin.

"I'll bet that's a hunting lodge," said Chris. "Let's see if anyone's inside."

They climbed up the porch, and knocked on the door, but there was no answer. Chris peered into a window.

"Okay, hold it right there!" came a gruff voice from behind.

They turned to see a tin soldier boy in a blue uniform pointing a rifle straight at them. "Don't you dare move, or I'll shoot. Are you friend or foe?"

"Friend, I think," said Chris.

"Drop your weapons!" Tin Soldier demanded.

"We don't have any," replied Chris.

"Hands up! I'll have to search you to be sure." Tin Soldier approached and frisked them. "Now empty your pockets!"

Chris did as he was ordered. "See? No weapons."

"Where are you from?" asked Tin Soldier.

"It's hard to explain," started Chris. "We're from outside Arboria. A magic ornament called Gabriel's Magic Ornament helped us get here."

"So you're a foreigner?" stated Tin Soldier sternly. "That means you are an enemy."

"We don't mean you any harm," said Laura.

"You'll have to prove it," demanded Tin Soldier. "If you are friends, you will assist in our war effort."

"War effort?" Chris stated. "What war are you fighting?"

"You must be joking," said Tin Soldier. "Everybody knows about the war. It's been going on for at least a hundred years."

"We didn't know that," said Chris. "Who are you fighting?"

"The Reds, of course. They're our enemy. They've always been our enemy. I can't believe you're so ignorant of world events."

"What's the reason for the war?" asked Laura.

"The Reds are our enemy. Do we need a better reason than that?"

Chris and Laura looked puzzled.

"Now," said Tin Soldier. "Choose a side, Blues or Reds. You'd better make the right choice if you want to live."

"Blues," said Chris. "But we haven't any reason to fight the Reds."

"You sound like one of those infernal doves," Tin Soldier said sternly. "They fly around trying to convince people not to fight. 'Listen to reason', they blubber. 'Try to solve your differences'. I'd love to shoot them all. You may not have a good reason to fight yet," said Tin Soldier. "But just wait. You will. Come with me. I need you both to help us make ammunition."

Tin Soldier led them to a workshop furnished with benches, tables, and tools. Mistletoe branches hung from the rafters, drying. On a table sat cans of mistletoe berries.

"That mistletoe is poisonous," Laura stated. "It can kill you."

"Of course it can kill you," said Tin Soldier. "That's WHY we make weapons from it."

"What kind of weapons do you make?" asked Laura.

"Arrows out of mistletoe branches and bullets out of berries," he replied. "I'll show you how it's done."

Tin Soldier showed Laura how to remove the berries from the branches and pack them into the cans. Then he showed Chris how to whittle arrows from the mistletoe branches.

"Don't cut your fingers," said Tin Soldier. "Remember you're working with poison." Then he told them, "I have to make a delivery to the front now. I'll be back soon. I'll know then whether or not I can trust you. If I find I can, I might let you go with me some time to the front. But you've got to prove yourselves first. If you do well, you'll be rewarded handsomely. If you don't, you'll be shot as traitors."

Tin Soldier then departed.

"I don't want to make weapons that could hurt anyone, do you?" Laura asked Chris.

"No," he answered. "But it can't be worse than cutting sugar cane."

"They don't even know why they're fighting," Laura said. "I don't think I'm going to like making weapons for them."

They had been sitting there for some time filling cans with berries and whittling arrows when they heard fluttering noises and discovered a white dove perched in the rafters.

64

"You are not in uniform," he cooed. "Why not?"

"We've just arrived," replied Laura. "They haven't issued us uniforms yet."

"A good thing," Mr. Dove replied. "I hope you refuse to wear them. What are you doing?"

"Making ammunition," Chris answered.

"That is bad. You are for their war, then, and not for peace?" Mr. Dove asked.

"We're not really for war," replied Chris. "We're not sure why there's one going on. We just volunteered to help Tin Soldier Boy."

"Believe me. There's no reason for their war," Mr. Dove stated. "I know why it started. Years ago, two brothers, Jack and Ned, got in a fight. Jack wouldn't let Ned play with his new toy rifle, so Ned broke it on purpose. Jack became so angry he broke Ned's bow and arrows. One thing led to another, and the boys grew up to be bitter enemies. Eventually, their children and grandchildren kept the fight going, shooting and destroying each other's property. The fight became so bad that everybody got involved. Now so much time has gone by, they don't even remember why they're fighting. They have completely forgotten the original reason for the war, and the original reason was not good enough to start their war in the first place. War has unfortunately become a way of life here now. The Blues and the Reds fight for the sake of fighting and for no other reason."

"That's too bad," said Laura. "Why can't they make peace?"

"Heaven knows, we've tried to convince them to do that," cooed Mr. Dove. "But making peace is a dangerous business. Many doves have been shot trying to get them to the table to talk about their differences. But the cause seems quite hopeless. The soldiers in fact seem to be getting meaner all the time. Now, when they see a dove, they shoot without thinking. We have become 'the third enemy' in the battle."

"That's terrible," said Chris.

"Another terrible result of their endless fighting is that they are ruining the land," Mr. Dove said. "Look out at the fields and see what I mean." Chris and Laura went to the door and looked out. "Deep, black holes are everywhere," Mr. Dove continued. "We call them hate-holes. The holes are dangerous, too. Children may never be able to play in the fields again."

"How very sad," Laura commented.

Suddenly Mr. Dove heard Tin Soldier returning. "I must go or end up as somebody's dinner," he said. "My advice? Do not join the war effort, no matter how strong the urge may be to do it. Have courage and stand up for peace as long as you can. If you children take a stand, maybe the war will come to an end. You could be the only hope." As Tin Soldier entered the shed, Mr. Dove fluttered off.

"What was that?" shouted Tin Soldier. "A dove? What did he tell you? Did he fill you full of lies?"

"I don't think he meant any harm," said Laura. "He tried to convince us that there is no good reason for your war and that you should try to make peace with your enemies."

"That makes me very angry," shouted Tin Soldier. "I wish I had come sooner."

"I don't understand why you hate the doves so much," said Chris. "They're only trying to help."

"You've let that ridiculous creature poison your mind," said Tin Soldier. "Their simple solutions won't work. Forget everything that birdbrain said. Now, show me how much have you done."

Tin Soldier examined the cans of mistletoe berries and the arrows Chris had whittled.

"Not so bad," he said. "I'm sure you would have done better if that idiot bird hadn't intruded. Anyway, I've been told by the Lieutenant to issue you uniforms as your reward. Soon you will be trained to fight. Then, if you become war heroes, you'll be given ribbons."

"Do girls have to fight?" asked Laura.

"Don't you want to fight?" Tin Soldier returned.

"Not really. I'm not very good at it."

"Will you be happy to let your brother become a war hero while you make ammunition?"

"I don't want my brother to fight either," said Laura. "I don't want him to get hurt."

Chris didn't want Tin Soldier to think he was a coward, so he said, "Give me the uniform."

"You won't be sorry," Tin Soldier replied.

"When will I see Chris again?" Laura asked.

"You can see him when you bring ammunition to the front lines."

"Do you know what you're doing?" Laura asked her brother. "You might get shot and die. I don't want to be left alone in this place."

"I promise I'll be careful," Chris replied. "Maybe I'll be able to see you tomorrow."

After Chris hugged his sister goodbye, he followed Tin Soldier to the front. The sound of gunfire became louder and louder as they approached. Soldiers were screaming, and officers were shouting commands. Smoke hovered everywhere, and many more of the black holes dotted the battlefield.

"Quick! Into the trench!" shouted Tin Soldier. "Here's your ammo. You know what to do."

"What?" Chris asked.

"Shoot anyone wearing red, you fool!" shouted Tin Soldier. "Score enough and you'll become a hero."

As Chris sat in the trench, something struck him as odd. Not all the soldiers were tin. Some seemed human like himself.

"Shoot!" screamed Tin Soldier. "The Reds are advancing!"

Chris peered out of the trench and started firing. He hit a Red in the heart. He was a human boy like himself, and that made Chris sad. At first Chris thought the boy was dead, but a few moments later, the boy stood up. Now part of the boy's face gleamed like metal.

"Did you see that?" Chris shouted. "The red soldier I shot is turning into tin."

"How else can a soldier become a seasoned warrior?" returned Tin Soldier. "You must get shot several times to become top notch. Watch this and you'll see how it's done."

Tin Soldier immediately jumped out of the trench and ran toward the Reds, shooting as he ran. Chris watched as Tin Soldier took a bullet in his shoulder. Someone shot him again before he could crawl back into the trench.

"You're hurt!" shouted Chris. "I'll get a doctor."

"No!" Tin Soldier winced and said, "I'll bear it like a man. I'll get my revenge. Don't worry. I'll get 'em good. I'll be a hero then. I'll get the ribbons I deserve."

Then something happened to Tin Soldier. He seemed even more metallic and less human than before—more like a machine than a human being.

"Are you sure you're okay?" Chris asked him. "I could get help."

"NO! I SAID!" With that Tin Soldier hopped out of the trench and ran into the midst of the gunfire, shouting, cursing, and shooting as many Reds as he could. Chris sat back in the trench, his eyes wide with disbelief. Then Tin Soldier fell. When Chris scrambled out of the trench and crawled to help him, Tin Soldier popped up and ran toward the enemy, shooting and yelling. Then in a snap, he exploded like a bomb.

When the smoke cleared, only a gigantic hole remained, and Chris recalled Mr. Dove's words about hate-holes. Just then a bullet pierced Chris's leg. He realized at once that a mistletoe berry had lodged there, so he ran for cover. The pain in his leg was terrible. When he examined it, he saw that the flesh around his wound was starting to turn to tin. Hatred for the Reds suddenly surged up inside him causing Mr. Dove's words to evaporate from his memory. He immediately started shooting at the Reds. He had been firing on the enemy for some time when he heard Laura's voice. This was something he did not expect. He jumped up and yanked her into the trench.

"What in blue blazes are you doing here?" he screamed.

Laura immediately noticed something different about him. "Chris, what have they done to you?"

"They've shot me! That's what!" He showed her the place in his leg that had turned to tin. "But I'm going to get them back. Now I have a reason to fight."

"Where is Tin Soldier?" asked Laura.

"He exploded," Chris said sadly, and then he began to sob. "They destroyed him. See that black hole? That's all that's left of him. I've got to fight for his honor. He was my friend. I must fight to avenge his death."

"Chris, don't you know what's happened?" Laura asked him. "You've been poisoned by one of Lesnit's mistletoe berries. We've got to get you to a doctor before it's too late."

"Get out!" shouted Chris. "This is no place for you. Leave me to fight."

Laura tried and tried to convince Chris to come with her, but he refused. She finally broke into tears, jumped out of the trench, and ran back to the cabin, frequently wiping her tears so that she would not trip along the way. She kept calling for Mr. Dove, hoping that he would appear and help her. "Please, Mr. Dove. My brother is hurt. You've got to do something." She sat on a log weeping for some time when she heard Mr. Dove cooing in a tree above her. She looked up and saw that he had an olive branch in his beak. Mr. Dove flew down, placed the branch in Laura's hand, and told her that she was to take the branch to Chris. He assured her that its oil would heal her brother's wounds.

With renewed hope, Laura ran back to the trenches as fast as her legs would carry her. When she arrived, she discovered that Chris had received several more wounds. Now his whole body seemed to be turning to tin. She could hardly bear to look at him in this condition.

"Chris, I have something to heal your wounds."

"I'll bear them like a man!" Chris shouted at her coldly. "That's the only way to be a warrior! Go away and leave me be!"

"Please," Laura begged. "Mr. Dove said your hatred will make you explode. You will turn into a hate-hole. Mr. Dove gave me this. It's the only thing that can help you."

"GO AWAY, I SAID!" Chris screamed. But Laura would not leave him. Instead she squeezed oil from the branch and sprinkled it on Chris's head and wounds. At first Chris was furious that she had done this, but soon, as his wounds began to heal, he became relaxed and fell asleep. After about an hour, Chris had returned to normal.

"Chris, wake up," Laura said, shaking him.

He opened his eyes. "Laura. Where are we?"

"You were under Lesnit's dark spell," she informed him. "You got hit with some of the mistletoe bullets. See what happens to soldiers when they are wounded and don't use this medicine? They turn into tin machines that hurt and destroy and then blow up like bombs. Lucky for us Mr. Dove had a remedy and you're okay."

"Thanks, Laura, you saved my life," Chris said. "I'm sorry I didn't listen to you in the first place. Let's get out of here."

They left the trench and headed back toward the cabin. When they arrived, they heard Mr. Dove cooing. "I'm glad you persuaded your brother to use the olive branch as medicine. Many soldiers don't have someone who cares about them like you care about your brother. Now that Chris is okay, I must be going. Others may agree to take my medicine before it's too late." After these words, Mr. Dove flew away, and Chris and Laura returned to the wood where

Lady had left them. Before long, they could see twelve stars circling above them. They were grateful that Lady was returning.

—Chapter Six—

SANTAS, SANTAS EVERYWHERE, BUT JUST ONE YOU CAN TRUST

WHEN LADY REJOINED the children, she said, "You have now seen firsthand how Lesnit has poisoned Arboria with selfishness and greed. Everywhere he goes, he makes bottomless pits appear. His apples make the Orna folk hungrier and hungrier until his terrible black holes swallow them alive. His mistletoe causes hate to swell up inside the tin soldiers until they explode and turn into hate-holes. Thus far, you have seen past Lesnit's trickery, but I warn you. The next land is Upper Arboria, and Lesnit will do his best to deceive you. His poison works there as much as in the other lands, so you must be on your guard."

As the children landed on a hill, Lady disappeared again. Light glittered from the snow-covered land. In the valley below, an old village was snuggled amid evergreen trees that wore gowns of icy lace. And yet the village was awake, for below the cold, silent gleam of snow-covered roof tops, windows glowed invitingly with warm yellow light. Beyond the village a star shone so brightly and beautifully that it caused joy to well up in the children's hearts when they beheld it.

As they walked toward the village, the children heard singing and laughing. In the distance, they could see a group of little people skating on a frozen lake. Chris and Laura thought they were children until they came closer and discovered they had pointy ears. They were elves!

"Hello!" Chris shouted, running toward them. Laura followed close behind him.

As he arrived at the frozen lake, an elf glared at him. "What are you doing here in Upper Arboria? You don't have pointy ears. Human children are not allowed. How did you get here?"

"Lady brought us," replied Chris.

"She could be a witch!" the elf declared to one of his fellows. "Out to sabotage our operation!"

"No!" said Laura. "She would never do that."

"You can't be sure," replied the elf. "Even in upper Arboria, odd characters lurk about. The other day an old codger was claiming to be Santa Claus. Imagine that! And at the North Pole no less!"

"The North Pole?" remarked Laura. "We thought this was Upper Arboria."

"That's one name for it," the elf said. "It's called North Pole, too." He said this in a way that made Laura feel stupid.

"What did the real Santa do about the old codger?" Chris asked.

The elf looked puzzled. "What?"

"What did the real Santa do about the fake Santa?"

"You poor, confused child," the elf replied. "There is no real Santa. People here haven't believed Santa was real for years now."

"Is he dead?" Laura asked sadly.

"How could he be dead when he never really existed?" the elf replied coldly.

Laura was almost in tears when she spotted a large man alighting from a carriage. He wore a red suit with white trim, a red cap, and had a long white beard. "There!" she shouted. "There he is! There's Santa Claus!"

The elf turned as three more large men, all looking like Santa Claus, got out of the carriage.

"Oh, them?" he said without a hint of surprise. "There are hundreds of them here. Not one of them is really Santa Claus."

"I don't believe you," Laura stated. "I want to find out the truth."

When the Santas returned to their carriage, Laura shouted, "Wait! May we ride with you? We need to ask you some questions." The Santas seemed reluctant, but they agreed. As the children climbed into their carriage, they smelled cologne. The fragrance was vaguely familiar.

"How did you get here?" asked one Santa. "You're not supposed to be at the North Pole."

"Lady brought us," replied Chris.

"Lady? Lady, who?" a second Santa Claus asked with a snicker.

"Probably a witch," replied a third.

"Oh, no. She couldn't be a witch," declared Chris. "She's too good and kind."

"Please," begged Laura, "we're looking for the real Santa Claus. Where can we find him?"

The Santas smirked, revealing fake beards. Their suits, which were made from cheap material, were coming apart at the seams. In places, the imitation fur was falling off as well.

"An elf told us there is no real Santa, but we didn't believe him," said Chris.

"We're on our way to a Santa Claus convention now," one Santa informed them. "Go with us and maybe you will find him there."

The other Santas chuckled when the children agreed to go to the convention.

Along the way, they passed through an old village. Ancient cobblestone streets led past houses and shops. Warm yellow light glowed in the windows and shone out onto the freshly fallen snow. Busy workers could be seen inside the shops and houses making toys and wrapping gifts.

"This must be where Christmas presents come from," Chris observed.

One Santa smiled and said to the others. "You see? The children believe this is real. That's all that matters."

"True," replied a second Santa. "Appearances are everything."

"Are you saying none of this is real?" asked Laura.

"If you want it to be real, it will be real for you," said a third Santa. "Enjoy it while you can. The older you get, the more the magic will wear off."

His words made Laura feel sad.

The carriage soon arrived at a town hall. Gathered in the square were hundreds of Santas, laughing, talking, and eating Christmas goodies. When the children stepped out of the carriage, they saw the star again.

"Look up there!" Laura exclaimed. "Isn't that the most beautiful star you've ever seen?"

"Oh, that old thing?" one of the Santas responded. "I almost forgot it was even up there. We are so used to seeing it, we hardly think about it anymore."

Before long, a Santa mounted a platform in front of the town hall.

"There," said Laura, pointing at him. "Could he be the real Santa?"

Another Santa overheard her and laughed. "If you want him to be the real one, then he'll be real for you."

The Santa on the platform began, "Mer' Xmas, fellow magicians."

Without enthusiasm, the Santas mumbled back, "Mer' Xmas."

"Did he say magicians?" Chris asked one of the Santas they'd ridden with.

"Of course," he replied. "We're all magicians, every last one of us."

"I thought you were all Santa Clauses," said Chris.

"Santas are magicians," he said, pulling a rabbit out of his sleeve, "masters of illusion!"

The Santa on the platform continued, "Allow me to introduce myself. My name is Jannes, and this is my twin brother, Jambres. Our Uncle Balaam is here today, too. You elected us to represent you on the North Pole Council, and we've been working very hard all year to make changes in our Constitution and Bylaws. We've finally purged from the books all outdated rules and regulations. We never followed the old rules anyway, so it's time that we changed them to reflect our new practices. My brother Jambres will explain why we've thrown out the so-called 'Naughty and Nice' policy. Jambres, come."

Jambres began, "Mer' Xmas."

"Mer' Xmas," they echoed back without enthusiasm.

"As you know, this policy states that only nice children will get toys for Christmas, while naughty children should expect nothing. For centuries this empty threat has been held over the heads of children. But when has it ever been carried out? Does anyone remember a child getting a 'rock in a sock'? This is why the North Pole Council has decided on a policy change. We have voted unanimously to do away with the 'Naughty and Nice' policy by removing it from our Constitution and Bylaws. This means it will be totally legal now to give presents to children, regardless of whether they've been naughty or nice."

The Santas applauded. Chris smiled and said to Laura. "That sounds like a great idea to me."

Jambres continued. "If this practice is followed at Christmas, it might be true for the rest of the year as well, so that children will never be denied anything. Isn't it our concern that children always be happy?"

The Santas applauded with shouts of "Ho! Ho! Ho!"

Jambres continued. "As you might expect, with good news comes a little bad news. Uncle Balaam will come and explain our new cost-cutting measures."

"God bless you," hollered Balaam, holding out his hands. "God bless you every one." The Santa Clauses laughed, but Chris and Laura couldn't figure out why.

Balaam continued, "I'm glad my nephew, Jambres, has explained our need to change the 'Naughty or Nice' policy. I'm in full agreement. However, this presents us with another problem. If we are now going to give presents to children whether they deserve them or not, we shall have to deal with the costs of making extra toys. I suggest we give cheaper gifts."

The Santas looked disappointed.

"That doesn't sound like such a good idea," Laura whispered to Chris.

Balaam held up his hands to signal quiet. "I know this goes against our tradition. But before you say it's a bad idea, let me remind you of some past mistakes when expensive gifts were thoughtlessly given to children. You remember the story of long ago about how three of our number, claiming to be 'Wise Men' following that silly star up there, once gave very costly gifts of gold, frankincense, and myrrh to a child who was barely a year old. Now this child had been born to peasant people, in a stable amongst animals no less! So I ask you. Could such a child appreciate the value of such gifts? I say no. Those magicians would have been wiser to give the child cheap toys. Most children tire of Christmas presents after they've played with them for a week or two anyway. Doesn't it make better sense to give children the cheapest toys possible? That way nobody will get upset when a child breaks a toy or loses interest in it. In my experience, most children prefer cheap toys anyway. So why not give the children what they want and save money at the same time?"

All the Santas applauded except for one who whispered to Chris and Laura, "Can you believe it's come to this? It's a sad day, isn't it?"

When they turned, they saw that this Santa was tall and slender and not dressed like the others. His beautiful red and green velvet cape, embroidered with gold thread, was a bit shabby. But unlike the other Santas, his beard and the fur on his suit were genuine, not artificial. He also wore a pointed red, green, and gold bishop's hat that glittered with beautiful jewels.

"I don't know why these magicians hark back to their old magic," he continued. "It has never worked." Somehow Balaam overheard him and said. "Be quiet, old fool. Everyone knows you're an eccentric impostor. Nobody takes you seriously."

The tall Santa just bowed his head and walked away.

"Who was that?" Chris asked.

"Don't mind him," one of the Santas said. "He's a loony, old magician who thinks he's the real Saint Nicholas. Calls himself the Bishop of Myra," Balaam said.

"The Bishop of Myra?" exclaimed Laura. "That's the one Dad said made Gabriel's Magic Ornament!"

A light went on in Chris's mind. "Of course!"

"So the Bishop of Myra is the real Saint Nicholas!"

"No, no, no, silly child," replied Balaam. "There is no such thing as a real Saint Nicholas."

"You don't know that," Chris said. "Come on, Laura. Let's go find out for ourselves."

"You're wasting your time," Balaam shouted as the children were leaving. "Our magic is all an illusion! Slight of hand! None of it is real! It's all a trick!"

—Chapter Seven—

NEXT STOP,
STAR AT TREE TOP!

"WAIT FOR US!" CHRIS SHOUTED. As he and Laura ran, they tried to keep sight of the bishop's hat on the tall Santa. When they finally caught up with him, Laura asked him breathlessly, "Are you really Saint Nicholas?"

He turned and smiled. "I mostly go by the name of Balthazar, though sometimes they call me the Bishop of Myra. I am really the Spirit of Giving. But you may call me Saint Nicholas if you wish."

"The other Santas say you're a crazy, old codger," Chris said. "They say you claim to be Saint Nicholas when there is no such person. Is what they say true?"

"Of course not," he replied.

"Then you are real," Laura declared. "Why don't they want us to believe it?"

"It's all part of the conspiracy to take the real meaning out of Christmas," he answered. "They may succeed in destroying it altogether if folks don't wake up. People like their magic because it's flashy and exciting. But their magic is bad. They practice it to create an illusion of goodness. I hate to say it, but those Santas and their leaders are rotten to the very core."

"One thing's for sure," Chris said. "Their plan to give cheap gifts to children doesn't sound good to me."

"Getting rid of the 'Naughty or Nice' policy is just as bad," Saint Nicholas told him. "That was a good policy. It helped teach children the value of gifts. But now that the gifts won't be valuable, I can understand why their North Pole Council has decided to do away with it. Why try to teach children the value of gifts that have no value?"

"It sounds to me like the work of Lesnit," said Laura. "The next thing you know, he'll be targeting the Star at Tree Top."

"You speak the truth," replied Saint Nicholas. "That is what Lesnit lives for, but I do not believe he will succeed. Look." He pointed at the star. "It shines as brightly now as it did on that night many years ago when I and my companions, Melchior and Casper, first saw it burning in the east and journeyed to see a young peasant child. Balaam referred to us as fools because we gave valuable gifts to the child. He doesn't seem to understand why we had to do it. It was the only way to quench the dark fires of greed and selfishness that burned in us all."

"You were one of the three Wise Men?" Laura inquired.

"In a manner of speaking," he replied. "I was the Spirit of Giving in the Wise Man Balthasar. But we weren't too wise before we found the Star. Had it not been for that Star, we would have remained foolish, evil magicians like Jannes,

Jambres, and Balaam. We would have kept leading people astray and weaving illusions with our false magic. Many of the Santas still do this because they have forgotten the Star. They ignore it although it holds the secret to true and lasting magic. I know why they ignore it, too. True magic takes a great deal of work and is more difficult to practice. False magic is easy to practice, but it can never really make people happy. There is little true magic left in Arboria, I'm sad to say. I hate to think what the future holds for this world. You have seen how much of Arboria Lesnit has eaten away or poisoned."

"Can you show us the true magic now?" asked Chris.

"Dear boy. True magic can't just be shown to a person all at once. Some people take a lifetime to understand and appreciate it. Since you have asked, however, I will try to help you see it. That's why you were brought to Arboria, after all." Saint Nicholas reached into his pocket, pulled out two pairs of spectacles, and handed them to the children. "These will help you tell the difference between what is real and what is illusion. Put them on."

When they did, they saw a golden angel standing in place of Saint Nicholas. The angel looked exactly like Gabriel's Magic Ornament, only larger. They removed the spectacles, and there Saint Nicholas stood again.

"How did that happen?" Chris exclaimed.

"Did you see a golden angel, too?" asked Laura.

"Yes," Chris replied.

"The spectacles help you see beyond the way things appear," said Saint Nicholas. "But I must warn you. Don't wear them until I say so. Otherwise, you might draw attention to yourselves. We must return now to the Santa Claus convention. I want to show you what's really going on there."

The children followed Saint Nicholas back to the convention where Jannes and Jambres were dancing on the platform with large, fancy canes and were singing a strange song.

"Be careful, children," warned Saint Nicholas. "What you see through the spectacles may frighten you. Be brave and try to show no fear. You may put them on now."

Chris and Laura were not prepared for what they would see. Instead of Jannes and Jambres, they saw two evil-looking men in black robes dancing with serpents and casting spells. The other Santas, when viewed through the spectacles, looked like big apples with bites taken out of them.

"Now I know what that cologne we smelled on the Santas was," Chris stated. "It was the odor of Lesnit's apples!"

"Exactly," said Saint Nicholas, who again looked like the golden angel. "Watch carefully. See how they are being eaten by the worms of greed and selfishness. I told you they were rotten to the core."

The children looked at the apples. Snakelike worms writhed and slithered through them.

"Now you see those Santas for what they are. Lesnit's evil magic infects them. It has now reached the highest region of Arboria. Now he slithers toward the Star at Tree Top in hopes that he can devour it. If he succeeds, he might destroy the true magic forever, and Arboria will fall under the spell of darkness and death. Come, children, we must journey quickly to the Star atop Arboria to learn the plan of Tree King who dwells there. He is the source of the true magic and the only one who can stop Lesnit's spell. Prepare yourselves for this last, dangerous stage of your journey."

After Saint Nicholas and the children left the assembly of evil magicians, he led them toward the Star. The children wore their spectacles, and Saint Nicholas still appeared as the golden angel. As they trudged through snow, he told them things that they needed to know for their journey.

"Till now, your guide has been Lady, but now I will guide you. Soon you will see stairs spiraling toward the Star."

"Where is Lady?" Laura asked.

"She is in the wilderness below Arboria preparing for battle with the evil serpent Lesnit."

"Why does she have to battle him?" asked Chris. "Can't Tree King do it?"

"Tree King could easily do it just by showing his face," replied Saint Nicholas. "But this would destroy not only Lesnit. It would also destroy Arboria, for no one can look upon the face of Tree King and survive."

"I'm afraid," said Laura. "What if we see his face accidentally?"

"He is good and kind, and would not deliberately hurt you. He will hide his face from you for that reason. You must take him seriously, however, for he is not to be trifled with."

As they made their way toward the Star, its brilliance became almost blinding. In its light the snow sparkled and glistened like diamonds set in golden pavement. Directly beneath it, the children saw a winding, golden staircase spiraling upward into the sky. At the foot of the staircase, a candle burned with golden light, and a bright, fiery gold liquid cascaded down the stairs like water rippling over stones in a brook.

"Give me your spectacles," said Saint Nicholas. "You will no longer need them. Take off your shoes and socks as well."

"Go barefoot in the snow?" exclaimed Chris. "Our feet will freeze!"

"The golden stairs will warm them," said Saint Nicholas. "You could try to climb the stairs with your shoes on, but you will find it impossible."

Chris took one step, but the stair gave way under the weight of his shoe, and he stepped into the snow beneath. He tried again using his bare feet.

"Wow, the steps are warm," Chris exclaimed. "But my feet feel strange; I feel like I'm walking on air."

"This golden stream must explain it," said Laura. "My feet feel as light as feathers."

90

"Is it hard to keep your balance?" Chris asked his sister.

Laura placed her left foot on the next step. "Yes. I feel so top heavy. My feet keep getting ahead of the rest of me, too."

"This is so weird," Chris remarked. "How will we ever get to the top?"

"Don't give up," replied Saint Nicholas. "You will find it gets easier as you climb. Don't watch your feet or think about how hard it is, for that will slow you down. Indeed, you might even lose your balance and fall. Keep your eyes fixed on the Star. That is where your help comes from."

As they climbed, the fiery, golden liquid became deeper and deeper. Soon it was up to their knees.

"Is there a reason the stream gets deeper?" asked Laura.

"It is preparing you to enter the Star; soon it will be over your heads."

"Won't we drown?" asked Chris.

"No," replied Saint Nicholas. "The stream of light will wash away the dirt of Arboria. Notice that your trousers have already turned white. The stream has washed them clean."

"That's wild," said Chris.

"Look at me!" exclaimed Laura. "My legs are turning white. And my skin is glowing like a light bulb. Is the golden water going to hurt me?"

"No," replied Saint Nicholas. "Keep climbing. You must go through the stream before entering the Star."

Chris pulled up his trouser leg. "Look, Laura, my skin is turning white, too. And my legs feel lighter than air."

"Mine, too," replied Laura. "I feel strangely clean on the inside, too, just like on the outside."

"You are forgetting to climb," Saint Nicholas said, reminding them. "You have not noticed that you have slowed down because you have taken your eyes off the Star. You must keep focused on it if you are to reach it. That is the place of true magic."

As they continued to climb, they kept passing more candlesticks. Each one looked like the one they had seen earlier. There were seven in all, spaced evenly along the winding stairs.

"What are the candles for?" Chris asked.

"Before the Wise Men found the Star of Bethlehem that now burns at Tree Top, they used seven candles to guide them in their magic. But the light of the candles was unpredictable. Their flames kept burning out, leaving Arboria in darkness. Then, in the midst of one winter, all seven burned out, leaving darkness everywhere. The hearts of the magicians turned evil, and their magic became black. Had Tree King not relit the candles during that dark winter, there is no telling what might have happened. True magic might have perished from Arboria forever."

"Could the candles go out again?" Laura asked.

"They haven't done so in a very long time," replied Saint Nicholas. "The light of the Star at Tree Top is the eighth and most glorious. It keeps the others lit so they will continue to burn."

"But if the candles no longer burn out, how come the Santas still practice their bad magic?" Laura asked.

"They choose to ignore the Star at Tree Top," Saint Nicholas replied. "They ignore the Star because they are too lazy to learn its true magic. Instead they keep returning to the bag of tricks they know so well. You've heard of their bag of tricks I presume?"

Chris and Laura shook their heads.

"I'm surprised Lady didn't tell you how Eva Isha Adams and her husband let the serpent Lesnit out of the bag he was in at Tree Bottom."

"Oh, yes," Laura responded, "she did tell us about that."

"That's the same bag of tricks the bad Santas use when they do their false magic," Saint Nicholas explained. "No matter how much light Tree King sheds on Arboria, there are some who insist on going back and fumbling through Eva Isha Adams's bag, as if it had something of value in it. That's the bag the Santas get the cheap toys from. Those gifts can never satisfy. They will only make children want more and more. No, the magic from these bags cannot satisfy anyone. Only magic from the guiding Star can fill a person with the light and joy of Christmas. We must press forward to the Star and see where it leads."

The golden liquid was now up to their necks.

"My heart feels warm and good," said Laura.

"Mine, too," said Chris. "Does the fiery, golden liquid make us feel this way?"

"Yes," Saint Nicholas replied. "Have you noticed yet where the stream's source is? It is gushing out of the Star at Tree top like a fountain. The golden stream is now filling your hearts with the joy of Christmas. But there's still the matter of your heads. The steam of light will have to flow over them so that your minds can be filled with the meaning of Christmas."

—Chapter Eight—

BITING OFF MORE
THAN HE CAN CHEW

THE STREAM OF LIGHT was soon up to Laura's chin and Chris's shoulders, but the stream did not slow them down like rushing water normally does when one tries to wade through it. In fact, their bodies now felt as light as a feather, and they were more in control of their movements than they had been when they were at the foot of the golden stairs. Indeed, now only their heads still seemed heavy.

"I'm scared," Laura panicked. "I might be able to put my head under the golden stream, but I'm afraid I won't be able to hold my breath for very long."

"You won't need to hold your breath," said Saint Nicholas. "The fiery liquid is not like regular water. It will not drown you. It will, however, take a bit of getting used to. It may be a good idea to practice breathing the golden liquid before going any further. I'll show you how." Saint Nicholas put his head beneath the water. "You see, children," he said. "I'm breathing with no difficultly whatsoever."

The children tried following his example by putting their heads under the fiery stream of light, but Laura's head soon popped back out. "It's no use," she panted. "I can't breathe that stuff."

Just then, Chris shouted. "I did it! It was easy!" His head immediately went under again.

"You must try again," Saint Nicholas encouraged Laura. "Your brother has managed to breathe the light and so must you. Don't be afraid now. Just try."

Laura again put her head under. This time, Chris latched on to her. "You can do it, Laura. Give it a try."

"Let go of me!" she shouted. As the light rushed into her mouth, she found she could breathe it without any trouble. "Oh. I'm doing it. Yes! This is so cool!"

"I had every confidence you could manage it," said Saint Nicholas, who had joined them. "Now you are ready to enter the Star at Tree Top."

The children were now completely submerged beneath the stream. Their clothes and skin had changed to glowing white, making them look like angels. As they got closer to the Star, they could see the golden liquid gushing out of it from every side. They had never seen anything quite like it. And it seemed very strange, because the Star itself was now much smaller than it had first appeared. It was so small, in fact, that a little child could easily hold it in his hands.

"How will we ever be able to get inside it?" Chris asked.

"It looks little on the outside, I know," Saint Nicholas told him, "but on the inside it goes on forever. When you are inside, you can never find the end of it. Are you ready to go in?"

They nodded.

"Remember what I told you earlier about Tree King. You must take him very seriously, for although he is good and kind, he also has great and terrible power. It would be unfortunate if you acted foolishly while you are inside his palace."

"Now," said Saint Nicholas. "Join hands and form a circle around the Star."

In a flash, the children found themselves in a glorious place. Thousands of angels were singing. All the angels were of different colors. Some colors were familiar. But there were others they had never seen before.

"How beautiful!" Laura exclaimed. "I've never seen any colors like those before. What are they called?"

"I forget that you've never seen the colors of the super-spectrum before," Saint Nicholas replied.

"The what?" asked Chris.

"The super-spectrum," he repeated. "In Arboria, you saw only seven colors—the colors of the spectrum and their combinations. Those colors are drab compared to the ones here inside the Star. You've heard of infrared and ultraviolet of course?"

"Yeah," answered Chris. "We studied about those in science."

"Those are two colors of the super-spectrum you couldn't see in Arboria. But you can see them right there," Saint Nicholas pointed, "and there. Here inside the Star new colors that never existed before are always popping up!"

"Wow, that's unbelievable!" Chris exclaimed. "How come we can see these colors now when we couldn't see them in Arboria?"

"There are different degrees of color blindness," Saint Nicholas explained to him. "Some people see only black and white. Others see black and white with a tinge of brown. Still others see only the seven colors of the spectrum and their combinations. That's what you saw before you came here. Before coming inside the Star, you were still somewhat color blind. But now that your eyes have passed through the stream, you can see the new colors you were blind to before."

"The singing of the angels is so beautiful, too," said Laura with a big smile on her face. "I've never heard such wonderful music."

"I'm sure you haven't," Saint Nicholas agreed. "When you were in Arboria, you were tone deaf as well as color blind. Now you hear the angels sing in supersonic harmony. The best four-part harmony in the world sounds dull by comparison, don't you agree?"

"Yes," said Laura. "In how many parts can these angels sing?"

"Millions upon millions, and all in wondrous harmony," replied Saint Nicholas. "There are perhaps as many parts as there are voices, and more kinds of harmony here than anywhere in Arboria. Like the new colors that keep popping up, new harmonies are always being invented and sung."

"What are they singing about?" Chris asked.

"I forgot you've not yet learned the tongues of angels," Saint Nicholas apologized. "As with everything else angelic, they sing with a super-language more beautiful and expressive than any language below. They sing now of the Christ child's coming. Soon they will descend to sing to the shepherds down in Arboria. Lesnit's evil is so widespread there that the shepherds are discouraged. Their flocks are scattering, and wicked shepherds are leading the Orna folk astray. The Santas you saw are really wicked shepherds, while the snowman and the dove you met earlier are some of the good ones. The only things wicked shepherds know how to do is to steal and destroy everything good and to horde up the things they have stolen for themselves. That song the angels sing now is a new song—a song of glad tidings to Arboria. It is a message of peace and good will that will encourage the good shepherds and give them hope during this time of deep darkness."

"Will the good shepherds hear and see the angels?" asked Laura. "Aren't they color blind and tone deaf like we were?"

"Yes, they are unfortunately. But Tree King will give them special sight and hearing when their time comes to see and hear the angels' message, just as you received special sight and hearing when you passed through the golden stream."

"The angels are so very beautiful," marveled Laura. "They are all so different. But their colors form pretty patterns like the ones in a kaleidoscope."

"I guess you could call that a super-kaleidoscopic formation," Chris commented, smiling.

"Very well put," Saint Nicholas said. "You may also observe that they never repeat the same pattern twice. Well, enough of this discussion. We're not yet to our destination. We must hurry toward the angel choirs that surround Tree King's throne. Once there you will learn the true magic."

Saint Nicholas held the children's hands, and they flew into the center of the swirling and singing angel choirs. The deeper they went toward the center of the Star, the more beautiful the colors and the singing became. They could now feel the music vibrating through every inch of their bodies. The children were so overwhelmed that they wept for joy.

"We shall soon enter the throne room of Tree King," Saint Nicholas told them. "Far beyond the angel choirs who sing of the birth of the Christ child is a place of silence and mystery. Beyond that is the throne of Tree King guarded by four strange creatures. They will hide the throne and the one who sits upon it, for no beings, whether earthly or heavenly, may look upon Tree King and live. The four creatures will tell Tree King's story silently, though you will hear them speak to your minds. And you must use only your minds, not your mouths, to speak to the strange creatures. Do you understand?"

The children nodded.

"Very well, the time has now come for me to leave. You must enter the place of silence alone."

"Please come with us," begged Laura. "I'm frightened."

"I am not needed where you are going," replied St. Nicholas. "Have courage, and you will be fine."

"Where exactly is this place of silence and mystery?" asked Chris. "How will we get there if we can't see it? And how do we get back?"

"Don't worry about that," St. Nicholas told him. "Just shut your eyes, block out all sound, and concentrate."

When they did as Saint Nicholas requested, they instantly found themselves in a place where they could not see but only could perceive with their minds. The first thing they perceived was a man dressed in a white robe and carrying a golden pitcher.

"Who are you?" the children wondered.

"I am a guardian of the Throne of Tree King," the Man conveyed with his thoughts. "Follow me, and I will tell you how Arboria came to be."

The children seemed to follow him without any feeling of movement. Below them, a tree spontaneously sprouted from barren ground. Filled with ornaments and lights, it looked like the Christmas tree in their home.

"Arboria was created by Tree King and no one else," the Man told them with his mind. "He is the maker of the universe, the creator. Lesnit is a destroyer, a maker of dark holes. We seek someone who can save Arboria from his destruction."

The Man disappeared and another creature emerged, an ox with golden horns and a hide as white as snow.

"Climb on my back and I will show you the battle for Arboria," the beast directed. The children obeyed and without feeling motion were carried to a place where they perceived three men with rods, one who was good, the other two who were wicked.

"Do you know them?" Chris heard the Ox ask. He recognized two of them. Laura thought they were Jannes and Jambres, the evil magicians.

"That is correct," said the Ox with his thoughts. "But the third man is someone you have not seen. Watch what happens when he throws down his shepherd's rod."

The children were stunned as the rod turned to a serpent. Jannes and Jambres changed their rods to serpents, too, and all the serpents began to fight one another. Then the first serpent swallowed the others. Its owner picked it up by the tail, and it turned back into a rod.

"Could that owner be an evil magician, too?" Chris wondered.

"No, he is a great deliverer who lived long ago," said the Ox. "He was sent to prove that the power of the King who made all things is greater than the power of all the evil magicians who ever lived. Long ago, he led slaves from bondage to freedom, just as you escaped from the sugarcane farms with Lady's help. Soon another great deliverer will come to lead the Orna folk from lower Arboria to the safety of the Star. But who will lead them out of their darkness? We must journey a bit further so that you can see the evil work of the third magician, Balaam."

They soon came to a man with his hands raised over a group of people in blessing. He seemed very sincere. Then the children realized he was Balaam. Laura and Chris began to think they may have judged Balaam too harshly.

"He is blessing them so they will trust him," the Ox indicated. "When they do so, he will turn on them. He will use his magic to deceive them and lead them back into the ways of evil. In the same way, the Santa Claus named Balaam will use his cheap gifts to draw attention away from the most valuable and best gifts. Children will be happy with his cheap gifts only for a little while. Who can reverse Balaam's dark spell?"

The Ox then left them and the children were greeted by a lion. Its fleece and mane were golden, its teeth were sharp as ivory swords, and its eyes were fierce and frightening. When the Lion spoke, Laura and Chris were terrified.

"Follow me," it said to their minds, "and I will show you how Arboria struggles."

The children followed him up a steep path that wound around a high Christmas tree. Atop the tree they could see the Star. It seemed now to be spewing out red fire and bellowing out smoke like a volcano. They heard a voice thundering, "Obey the rules. Submit to the laws."

Many Orna folk were on the lower branches. Some were trying to climb the branches, but few continued their struggle for long. They became tired and weary from the effort. Other Orna folk lost their grip and fell into the black holes.

"The Orna folk you see now no longer find joy in the Star," said the Lion. "They climb the branches out of duty to the voice. But is it really the voice of Tree King they hear?"

The children looked up at the Star and listened. They could hear angelic music, and they desperately wanted to climb the branches and enter the Star.

"See what I mean?" said the Lion, whose roar now was strong and comforting. "The struggle is difficult unless you keep your eyes on the Star. Remember how hard it was to climb the golden stairs unless you looked at the Star? It takes courage to reach the top. But who can give the Orna folk courage to climb?"

The Lion left them, and they saw a white eagle with a golden beak. "Come with me," called the Eagle, "and I will show you the death of Arboria."

"Death?" thought Laura. "Must Arboria die?"

"It has already begun to die," responded the Eagle. "Lesnit's power reaches now to the highest branches. Arboria's branches are dry and dead. Now, climb on my back."

The Eagle carried them upward on the wind until they could see the winding, golden stairs.

"Look," he said, "Lesnit is crawling up the stairs at Tree Top."

From the Eagle's back, the children could see the serpent slithering up the golden staircase, devouring the golden liquid from the stream of light. As it passed each candlestick, it made a sucking sound and snuffed their light out.

"He goes now for the Star at Tree Top!" the Eagle cried. "We will learn soon what Tree King plans to do about it when we gather around his throne."

The Eagle flew with the children back into the place of silence and mystery. The Man with the pitcher, the Ox, and the Lion had returned.

"Arboria has dried up and come to a miserable end," said the Man with the pitcher. "Lesnit, has drunk all water from the bottom of the tree. He has devoured every angel star. Who can stop him? Who can bring a new beginning to Arboria?"

"Arboria is suffering from the evil magic of Jannes, Jambres, and Balaam," said the Ox. "The dark holes of Lesnit swallow more and more selfish, miserable Orna folk. Who can turn the tide of battle?"

"The Orna folk have given up their struggle to reach the Star," said the Lion. "They found the way too difficult. They no longer have the desire or courage to go on. They are sinking into the dark pits. Who will give them courage? Who will give them strength to climb towards the light?"

"Arboria is dead!" cried the Eagle. "Only darkness and misery remain. Must Arboria perish? Who will help?"

Suddenly, Lady appeared. She seemed very sad, and the candles on her head burned dimly. "The battle beneath Arboria has begun," she said. "The time has come for Lesnit to try to devour the Star. He will try, but he will not succeed. Good cannot be destroyed. There is not much time now. Lesnit has already snuffed out the light from the candles on the golden stairs, and he is only a few steps from the Top Star. We must escape while we still can."

"You have been faithful in the battle," the Eagle told Lady. "Soon victory will be yours. I now lend you my wings, which you have earned because of your faithfulness to Tree King. Flee now with the children into the wilderness beneath Arboria. A place of safety awaits you there."

The Eagle gave Lady his wings, making her look altogether like an angel. She embraced the children and flew outside the Star at Tree Top. As they hovered, they could no longer see the winding, golden stairs. They could see only the blackness of Lesnit's body as it coiled upward. Terrified, they watched as Lesnit opened his mouth, lunged at the Star, and devoured it.

"Look what he's done!" Chris cried out.

"It's the biggest mistake he ever made," Lady said. "It will be his undoing. Just watch and listen."

The children looked on in stunned silence as the tree suddenly became a giant firework display. It crackled, hissed, and popped, emitting a blinding, flashing light. As the Star slid down Lesnit's throat, he looked like a string of firecrackers going off. The children tracked it as it slid down through his body. As it moved, it left behind a golden, glistening light. Soon, every inch of Lesnit's body from head to tail glittered and sparkled.

"It's just like the fireworks on New Year's Eve," said Chris. "Have you ever seen anything like it?"

"Lesnit is turning inside out," said Lady. "Isn't it wonderful?"

"What's happening to him?" Laura wanted to know.

"He's becoming a garland of tinsel," replied Lady. "Don't you know what Lesnit is spelled backwards?"

"Oh, I get it!" exclaimed Chris. "LESNIT is TINSEL spelled backwards!"

"That is so cool," Laura laughed.

"It's brilliant really," remarked Lady. "Tree King knew that Lesnit could not tolerate the Star. The Star may seem small on the outside, but you and I know that isn't the way it really is. The Star expands to an infinite size in every direction. That's something Lesnit just didn't count on, and it's the very thing that has brought about his demise."

"He really deserved it, too," Chris said with a look of satisfaction in his eyes.

"But what about Arboria?" Laura asked. "Lesnit has been turned into tinsel, I know, but is Arboria still going to be dead?"

"There is hope," said Lady. "On the Eagle's wings, I shall take you beneath Arboria to the very place where Eva Isha Adams and her husband first let Lesnit out of the bag. You will see something going on there that is extraordinary."

Lady carried them down until they reached a dark, empty place under the lowest branches of Arboria. She alighted in a very desolate place and released Chris and Laura from her embrace.

"We're in wilderness territory now," said Lady. "It may seem frightening here, but now it just so happens to be the safest place in all Arboria. As you can see, no gifts are under the tree. Do you know why?"

The children shook their heads, wondering what she could mean.

Lady led them to a large, ugly bag. It resembled the bags of the Milk Maids at the Partridges and Pears store in Lower Arboria.

"This is the bag that Eva Isha Adams opened with the help of her husband," Lady explained. "There have been no presents under the tree because Lesnit has hoarded every one of them up in this bag. Now that he has been defeated, though, it is safe to open the bag and look in."

"Are you sure we should peek?" asked Laura. "What if he escapes again?"

"Christmas day has come, so it is okay to peek now," Lady assured her. "Lesnit won't be able to escape because something very special has happened to the bag. Just open it and see what I mean."

Together, Laura and Chris opened it and peeked inside. As they did, a star flew out, almost hitting them in their heads. As it rose up through the branches of Arboria, ornaments of all kinds as well as the many angel stars Lesnit had devoured followed it.

"Do you understand what you've seen?" Lady asked them. "The first star that flew out of the bag is the Star Lesnit devoured at Tree Top. He didn't hurt it in the least. Now it rises to resume its place at Tree Top again. The angel stars Lesnit devoured are returning to their places, too. The ornaments will once again be guided upward through the branches of Arboria until they merge with the Star. Now I must take you inside the bag."

Lady and the children gradually became smaller. She gathered them in her arms, and they flew together into the bag. The angels they had seen inside the Star were there, and their singing and appearance now seemed more beautiful than ever. Below, they saw shepherds traveling down a road.

"This is the way Tree King plans to fill the greed and hate-holes Lesnit left behind. Tree King has given Arboria the most valuable gift of all. Come with me and I will show it to you."

The children followed Lady as she led them to a cave. They could hear animals inside—cows mooing, donkeys braying, ducks quacking, and chickens clucking. The next thing they heard was a baby cooing.

"The baby you hear could have been born to a king and queen in upper Arboria, you know," she told them as they approached the entrance of the cave. "But that would not have helped the dwellers in the regions here below to escape their misery. Instead he was born to common folk like the ones you're getting ready to see inside that cave. Curious people in Upper Arboria will no doubt come also when they learn what has happened here."

The children still did not quite understand what was happening. They kept looking for the valuable gift Lady had told them about. As she led them into the cave, they expected to find a treasure horde. They had after all always heard that dragons guarded treasures, and since this was Lesnit's former den, they expected to see gold, silver, and precious jewels. Instead, they only found the child they previously had heard cooing. Strangely, he was lying in a feed trough wrapped in rags. His mother and father, who looked like peasants, were sitting beside him smiling at him.

"This is interesting," Chris said. "But where is the valuable treasure?"

Lady did not answer but continued to look in the direction of the baby. Just then, they noticed the child's mother looked very much like Lady. They looked at Lady, then back at the child's mother, and then back at Lady.

Lady knew what they were thinking. "The time has come for me to tell you who I really am. I am the spirit of love in the mother of that child and in the heart of all those who have learned the meaning of the magic of love. The woman you see there is a grandchild of Eva Isha Adams, which means 'Eve, the wife of Adam'. This grandchild is the one I told you about earlier—the only one in Arboria who could help reverse Lesnit's spell. Through her and people like her, hatred and greed in the world will be turned inside out by deeds of love. I stand for all people of all times who have struggled against the evil serpent of greed and hatred to bring the love of this child to their hearts."

As they gazed upon the child, the children then saw Wise Men, bringing gifts of gold, frankincense, and myrrh. Now they understood who the child was. They would have guessed it earlier, but they were thrown off by the cave and the feed trough. Now, however, his identity was being confirmed by the arrival of the Wise Men. One of the Wise Men looked strangely like St. Nicholas, except that he was dressed very differently.

"Hey," said Chris. "Don't we know you?"

The Wise Man set his gift of gold before the Christ child and knelt down in worship. Then he turned to Chris. "I am Balthazar. You mistook me for Saint Nicholas because I have in me the Spirit of Giving just as he did. That Spirit sometimes appears as well as the angel Gabriel because he was the first to proclaim the gift of the child you see there. This was the greatest and most valuable gift ever given—the gift of love more valuable than this gold I have brought him."

Suddenly, Gabriel flew out of Balthazar's body and appeared to them. "Children, you see now the true magic of Christmas, the gift that makes all the other gifts underneath the tree possible. This is the magic that will bring Arboria back to life and fill the gaping holes of greed and hatred. Come see what is happening to Arboria. Light, love, and joy are spreading through the branches. There is light where there was once darkness, and rejoicing where there was once sadness. The golden angel took the children by the hand, and they flew together through Arboria.

"Look," said the Angel. "There are Fat Pig and Old Mutt. They are learning now to be friends. If you listen, you will hear them singing."

"They sound pretty bad," said Chris, remembering the perfect harmony of the angel choirs. "Can't they do better than that?"

"They're doing the best they can," the Golden Angel said. "They will get better in time."

"Oh, no," said Laura. "They're fighting again."

"I know it's discouraging," said the Angel. "They have a lot to learn. But the point is that they are learning to sing that song. The good news is that they will sing it to hungry people and give them food as well. At least this means Fat

Pig and Old Mutt will no longer be hoarding apples. And see?" he pointed. "There's Snowman."

"Oh, look!" shouted Laura. "He's not dirty anymore. I'm so happy. He was such a nice Snowman. But how did he get so clean?"

"He bathed in liquid from the golden stream."

"That's wonderful," said Laura.

They flew toward the department stores and the amusement park.

"Remember the way children were being made into merchandise here?" the Angel reminded them. "Well, the dolls have been changed back into children and have been returned to their parents. The parents have realized they were wrong to neglect their children. Parties and nice things are less important to them now. They have learned that such things cannot make them happy."

"What about the doll Lady bought me when we were there?" Laura inquired. "Was he changed back, too? That mean old Mr. Budgens took him from me, you know."

"Your doll is a child again and has been returned to his parents," replied the Angel. Things are very much better in this land, not perfect, mind you, but there's hope for greater and greater improvement. Now let's go up to the next land and see what's happening there."

"Do you recognize those people?" the Angel asked, pointing below.

"Yes," said Chris. "That's the awful Mr. Budgens and the mean Mrs. Margumont."

"Look closer at them."

"They're smiling," observed Laura, "and Mrs. Margumont's hair is lovely!"

"I know it's hard to believe," said the Angel. "Mr. Budgens and Mrs. Margumont were not always mean. They became bitter because they were lonely. They have fallen in love now. They've even decided to change their work farm into a home for unwanted children. The children will have chores to do, of course, but they will be well fed and well treated from now on."

"What about Jimmy and Sally?" asked Chris.

"They've learned their lesson about eating too much candy," replied the Angel. "They're glad they don't have to stuff themselves with sweets anymore."

The Angel carried Chris and Laura to the place where the tin soldiers had been fighting.

"Listen," he told them. "Do you hear anything unusual?"

"No," the children replied.

"You no longer hear the sound of gunfire, right? The reason is that peace has come. But the doves have work to do repairing the terrible damage. They are healing the wounds of the soldiers with the oil of their olive branches. The mistletoe, too, has lost its power to make people hate one another. Do you see what the doves are doing with it now?"

"They're tying it on trees and above doorways!" exclaimed Laura.

"You know what that means, right?" asked the Angel. "The mistletoe is now a sign of peace and love."

They flew upward toward the North Pole or Upper Arboria. The Santa Clauses were having another convention, but Jannes, Jambres, and Balaam were missing.

"What happened to the three evil magicians?" asked Chris.

"They were voted out," the Angel informed them. The Santas have learned what I knew all along. Namely, the old magic of lies and greed doesn't work. When the old Constitution and Bylaws were put back in place, Jannes, Jambres, and Balaam left in a huff. The 'Naughty or Nice' policy is back to stay as well, and Balaam's idea of giving cheap gifts to the children has been unanimously rejected. Soon I'll be returning here to help Saint Nicholas be their leader. With the evil magicians gone, Christmas will be quite safe again. Now come with me to Tree Top to look at the Star one last time."

As they flew upward, they saw the Star gleaming brighter than ever, and every one of the seven candles around the winding, golden stairs was lit as they had been before.

"Look, children, the Star of Bethlehem. It guides us to the true meaning of Christmas."

"It seems even more beautiful," observed Chris.

"The more one looks at it," replied the Angel, "the more beautiful it becomes."

Soon the Angel led them from Arboria to the real world. The children could see their mother and father standing as still as statues.

"Sadly, the time has now come for me to leave you," said the Angel. "Never forget this Christmas dream. Practice always the true magic of Christmas—the magic of love. Adults have problems understanding Christmas dreams, you know. So be patient with your parents if they don't believe you at first. Maybe with time you will help them understand what you have seen."

The Angel again became Gabriel's Magic Ornament and slowly vanished to return to the old church in the little town of Bethlehem from whence it had come.

—Chapter Nine—

NO DREAM CAN LAST FOREVER,
OR CAN IT?

"WELL HOW DO YOU LIKE THAT?" remarked Dad. "Those lights at the bottom of the tree just came back on by themselves. Now I won't have to replace them."

"Gabriel's Magic Ornament!" Chris shouted. "It disappeared just as Dad said it would!"

"I was only joking," said Dad. "Maybe the ornament has fallen off the tree."

"No," said Chris. "It was in our hands just a moment ago."

"We were both holding it," Laura added. "It really was a magic ornament. You were right. We had the most wonderful Christmas dream."

"That's nice," said Dad, smiling. "It's fun to make believe."

Chris frowned. "But it wasn't make-believe! It was real," he argued.

"It's the truth," Laura insisted. "We went first to a land where there was a pig and a dog fighting over apples, and we met a snowman. Only he was dirty because of an explosion

Lesnit made. He's the evil serpent. That's Lesnit I'm talking about, and..."

"Not so fast," Dad interrupted.

"Don't forget about Lady," said Chris.

"Oh, yes," Laura said. "She was so nice. She was our guide."

"We met the real Saint Nicholas, too," Chris said. "He led us into the Star at Tree Top where Tree King dwells."

"My goodness!" exclaimed Dad. "Where did you children get such imaginations?"

"Where do you think?" remarked Mom, looking at him and smiling.

"And the lights that went out at the bottom of the tree," said Chris. "Dad, do you know why they went out?"

"No, tell me."

"Lesnit ate them," the children said together.

"It's the truth," Chris tried to convince him. "Lesnit was the evil serpent who was let out of the bag by Eva Isha Adams. Lesnit ate the angel stars, and that's why the lights at the bottom of the tree burned out."

Dad smiled.

"You don't believe us, do you?" Laura said with a frown. "It happened while you and Mom were frozen. Lesnit ate the angel stars at the bottom of the tree. He did other terrible things, too. He made the people in Arboria turn mean. We even had to work on a sugarcane farm. It was awful. I got so scared."

"Arboria? Sugarcane farm?" Mom mumbled.

"But Mom and I weren't frozen," Dad said, laughing. "We've been here with you all the time."

"You don't remember being frozen?" Chris asked. "But of course you don't. It happened right before Laura and I started to shrink."

Dad looked at his watch. "It couldn't have been very long. Only a couple of minutes have passed since you and Laura put the ornament on the tree. How do you explain that?"

"I don't know," said Chris. He smiled. "Call it magic?"

"I guess so," Dad said. "Strange things happen all the time."

"Then you do believe us?" asked Laura.

"I'm trying to," said Dad.

Mom noticed the garland of tinsel on the tree. "When did you put that awful stuff on there?" she pointed. "You know I don't care for tinsel. It makes the tree look so...cheap."

The children laughed. They remembered that the Santa Clauses wanted to give the children cheap gifts. It served Lesnit right to be made into something cheap.

"I'm not the one who put it on," said Dad. "Did you?"

"No," the children replied.

"Well somebody did," Mom said. "And who put the manger scene under the tree? We've never had it there before."

"Beats me," said Dad.

"It wasn't there a minute ago, and neither was the tinsel," Chris tried to convince them. "That's what we've been trying to tell you. It's part of the magic."

"You've got to admit this is very strange," Mom said to Dad.

"Strange, but true," Laura assured her. "The best part of our dream, though, was that we learned the real magic of Christmas."

"What magic is that?" asked Mom.

"The magic of love," replied Laura. "Love is the real Christmas magic. Love filled the black holes of Arboria with light and joy. Love is the only magic worth practicing. A wise magician taught us that."

"A very wise magician," Mom repeated. She hugged Laura and Chris. "Well, I'll have to agree with that magician. If you learned that the true magic of Christmas is the magic of love, then your Christmas dream was truly worthwhile."

"Mom's right," said Dad. "Maybe next year Mom and I can take a trip into the Christmas tree!"

"That would be an adventure, to be sure," Mom said.

Later that evening, after the children were in bed, Mom and Dad searched for the magic ornament, but they did not find it. Mom was a bit upset with Dad because now he would not be able to return it for a refund. Mom and Dad did not realize that in some mysterious way, Gabriel's Magic Ornament had returned to the old church in Bethlehem from whence it had come. Something extraordinary had happened to their children, however, and it wasn't just their dream. Something about them had changed for the better. Though the years passed, Chris and Laura never forgot the magic ornament that made all their Christmases from that time forward special. They often related the dream Gabriel's Magic Ornament had given them, and for the rest of their lives they practiced the true magic of Christmas—the magic of love.

—THE END—

About the Author

RANDALL BUSH is a Professor of Philosophy and the former Director of the Interdisciplinary Honors Program at Union University in Jackson, Tennessee. An ordained Baptist minister, he holds a Bachelor of Arts degree from Howard Payne University in Brownwood, Texas; the Master of Divinity and Doctor of Philosophy degrees from Southwestern Baptist Theological Seminary in Fort Worth, Texas; a Doctor of Philosophy degree from the University of Oxford in England; and studied at the University of Texas; and for a brief time in Germany. For five years, he was a Professor of Bible at his college alma mater where he also served for one year as Vice President for Student Affairs. Upon returning from his doctoral studies in Great Britain, he served as Rockwell Visiting Theologian at the University of Houston before coming to teach at Union in 1991. He also taught ninth-grade English at Lamar High School in Houston, Texas, and served as an adjunct Professor of Philosophy in the Houston Community College and the North Harris County College systems. He is the father of two grown and married children, Chris and Laura, and now resides in Jackson, Tennessee with Cindy, his wife of 36 years.

Bush's other life experiences have included attending the Houston Conservatory of Music, playing first-chair first trumpet in his high school band, hymn-writing, extensive travel, doing mission work in the Houston inner city, living on a West Texas ranch, and serving as a part-time minister in a British Baptist church. He has also served numerous churches as a Sunday School teacher, a church pianist, a church organist, a minister to youth, a minister of music, a minister of education, and an interim pastor.

CPSIA information can be obtained at www.ICGtesting.com
Printed in the USA
LVOW031253301111

257157LV00003B/5/P